THE BEST
"FUNNY–BONE TICKLING"
JOKES EVER

K. Sabesan

iUniverse, Inc.
Bloomington

The Best "Funny-Bone Tickling" Jokes Ever

iUniverse books may be ordered through booksellers or by contacting:

iUniverse
1663 Liberty Drive
Bloomington, IN 47403
www.iuniverse.com
1-800-Authors (1-800-288-4677)

Because of the dynamic nature of the Internet, any Web addresses or links contained in this book may have changed since publication and may no longer be valid. The views expressed in this work are solely those of the author and do not necessarily reflect the views of the publisher, and the publisher hereby disclaims any responsibility for them.

ISBN: 978-1-4502-5897-5 (pbk)
ISBN: 978-1-4502-5898-2 (ebk)

Printed in the United States of America

iUniverse rev. date: 12/7/2010

School

The students were very noisy when the teacher entered the class. The teacher said, "Quiet everybody! Why are you all making so much noise?" One of the students said, "We found this twenty dollars and decided to give it to the person who tells the biggest lie." The teacher looked sternly at the student and said, "When I was your age I didn't know what "lie" was!" The student gave the teacher the twenty dollars.

*

Teacher: "Childhood is the best period in a person's life." Student: "Do you think so sir? I'm forced to go to bed when I'm wide awake and am forced to wake up when I'm fast asleep. I'm forced to eat when I am not hungry and worse still something that I don't like to eat."

*

A student found a wallet with a few hundred dollars in it and went to the principal's office and handed it over to him. The principal, touched by the student's honesty, told him, "You are such an honest boy and I truly appreciate what you have just done." He then asked, "There is so much money in this wallet. Tell me the truth, were you not tempted to keep the wallet?" Replied the student, "Yes, but another student saw me picking it up."

*

Teacher: "If I say, "I am beautiful", what tense am I using?" A student seated behind said softly, "Looking at your face it cannot even be considered a past tense!"

*

Teacher: "Today is April Fool's day. Anyone who thinks he's a fool, please stand up." After a while, one student stood up. The teacher asked, "Are you a fool?" Replied the student, "No, but I stood up just to keep you company." (Such a considerate student who couldn't bear to see his teacher standing all alone).

*

A mathematics teacher irritated with one of his students who kept on giving wrong answers for a simple mathematical problem, snapped, "John, for heaven sake, use your brains!" A student seated in the last row uttered, "How could he possibly use something he doesn't have!"

*

Teacher: "In which battle did Napoleon Bonaparte die?"
Student: "Napoleon Bonaparte died in his last battle."

*

Teacher: "What did Caesar say when Brutus stabbed him?"
Adrian: "Ouch"

*

Teacher: "Jeremy, can you please pay a little attention."
Jeremy: "Sir, I'm already paying as little as I can."

*

Teaching is a noble profession. When the teacher is teaching, the students love to tell the teacher, "Stop boring us to death, you idiot." But they can't.

*

Student: "Sir, money is countable and why do they say 'much money' and not 'many money'?"
Teacher: "Well, I won't be able to answer your question because it didn't occur to me to ask my teacher this question when I was a student."

*

Student: "Sir, why is phonetics not spelled the way it sounds?'
Teacher: "If it is spelled "fonetics" no one will know it is phonetics."

*

Student: "Sir, why isn't the number eleven pronounced as "onety-one"?"
Teacher: "If it is pronounced as "onety-one" no one will know it's eleven except you!"

*

Teacher: "Kelvin, can you please wake Moses up."
Kelvin: "Sir, it's not fair. You put him to sleep and you make me wake him up!"

*

Teacher: "What is the most popular answer to school teachers' questions?"
Student: "I don't know."
Teacher: "Correct."

*

Teacher: "What is a Gorilla Warfare?"
Student: "Gorilla Warfare is a war where monkeys throw coconuts at each other."

*

Mother: "John, wake up or you'll be late for school."
John: "I don't want to go to school, mummy, nobody likes me in school."
Mother: "John, I'm sick and tired of hearing this every morning from you. Now, out of bed and get ready to go to school. I hate to keep reminding you that you are the principal."

*

Mother: "Angie, your teacher said you are not paying attention in class."
Angie: "When I pay full attention with my eyes wide open to something which is extremely boring, I tend to doss off."

*

Student: "I didn't do my homework because I lost my memory."
Teacher: "When did it happen?"
Student: "When did what happen?"

*

Some schools don't engage cross-eyed teachers fearing that they might not have control over their pupils.

*

Why do teachers talk to themselves?
No. They are actually teaching but the students are not listening.

*

Why did the teacher wear sunglasses?
Because his students were very bright.

*

Student to Teacher: "My parents didn't punish me for something I didn't do at home. Will you punish me sir, if I tell you?"
Teacher: "Your parents didn't punish you, so why should I. Anyway, what is it?"
Student: "Sir, I didn't do my home work."

*

Teaching is a noble profession. Teachers teach and students have difficulty paying attention and end up having tuition at home.

*

Teacher: "Cleanliness is next to godliness."
Student: "With my little sister it's next to impossible."

*

Teacher: "If you had six chocolates and your friend asked for two, how many would you have left?"
School bully: "Six."

*

Teacher: "John, I give you four apples and then two apples. How many apples will you have?"
John: "Seven apples, sir."
Teacher: "John, listen carefully. I give you four apples and then another two. How many apples will you have?"
John: "Seven apples, sir."
Teacher: "John I want you to explain how you arrived at seven!"
John: "I already have one apple in my bag, sir."

*

Teacher: "Which month has 28 days and 29 days in a leap year?"
Student: "All the months."

*

The students in a particular school are so difficult to handle, the teachers play truant.

*

Teacher: "Why didn't you come to school yesterday?"
Student: "I was sick - sick of school."

*

John: "When do you like school best?"
Sam: "When it is closed."

*

Grandmother: "What does this 'F' mean in your report book?"
Grandson: "Fantastic".
Grandmother: "Oh my, I'm so proud of you my sweet darling."

*

Teacher: "John, how old are your father and mother?"
Student: "They are as old as I am."
Teacher: "How can they be your age?"
Student: "Because they became father and mother when I was born."

*

Teacher: "All those who wish to go to heaven please raise your hands."
All the children raised their hands except for little Eunice.
Teacher: "Eunice, don't you like to go to heaven?"
Eunice: "I'd love to but my mother said I should go straight home after school."

*

Teacher: "Why do they call the Middle Age the Dark Age?
Student: "There was no electricity then and there were too many knights."

*

Teacher: "Which is farther away? Canada or the moon?"
Adrian: "Canada."
Teacher: "Why do you say that?"
Adrian: "We can see the moon but we can't see Canada."

*

Physics teacher: "What is the difference between lightening and electricity?"
Isaac: "You don't have to pay for lightening."

*

Teacher: "What is water?"
Gregory: "Water is a colourless, odourless, tasteless liquid which you can drink, wash your hands, wash your plates and clothes, bathe, swim and get drowned."

*

Doctors

Why do doctors practise?
They practise or keeping practising to overcome their live threatening, near-fatal and fatal mistakes in order to become perfect one day.

*

What is the similarity and dissimilarity between a doctor and a lion?
Dissimilarity - A lion is ferocious and a doctor is not.
Similarity - Both are life-threatening.

*

Are doctors more live threatening than leopards, tigers and lions?
Yes, say some people because they are unlikely to encounter or face a leopard, tiger or lion in their entire live but they have no choice but to see a doctor when they are sick.

*

Family members wanted to take a sickly old man to the doctor. But the old man refused and said, "I would rather die a natural death!"

*

Why do doctors wear masks in the operating theatre?
To cover up their live threatening, near-fatal and fatal mistakes!

*

Why do nurses wear masks in the operating theatre?
To escape from being called up as a witness in any court trial involving any of the doctors they happened to be with in the operating theatre.

*

Doctor to patient: "I have good news and bad news for you."
Patient: "What's the bad news?"
Doctor: "Instead of doing it on the patient next door, we mistakenly amputated both your legs."
The patient almost fainted. He became hysterical and started screaming and hurling vulgarities at the doctor. He then cried uncontrollably. Those around him tried to calm him down. Once he had calmed down, he asked the doctor, "What's the good news?"
Doctor: "The hospital is not charging you for the amputation."

*

A patient who was about to undergo a major heart surgery asked the doctor, "Doctor, why is a fresh fragrant garland hung on the wall?" Replied the doctor, "If the operation is successful I wear it, if it is otherwise, you wear it."

*

Patient: "Doctor, my stomach pain is so unbearable, I feel like killing myself."
Doctor: "Oh no. You don't kill yourself, leave that to me."

*

Patient: "Doctor, I'm having difficulty breathing."
Doctor: "I can stop that."

*

Who are those who easily get away with murder? Doctors.

*

A nurse calling a doctor on the phone: "Doctor, we have a patient who met with an accident and his condition is very serious."
Doctor: "I can only reach the hospital in half and hour's time. Keep a close watch and if anything happens, not to worry, I'll be there on time to certify him dead."

*

A doctor was in love with an adorably beautiful girl. He mustered enough courage and wrote her a love letter. He waited for a few days but there was no response from the girl. He then called her to find out if she had received his letter. She told him that she threw his letter in the dustbin. Shocked, the doctor asked, "Why?"

She said, "Your letter was disgusting."

Puzzled, the doctor queried, "Disgusting?"

The girl: "You wrote a long letter but I couldn't read a single word."

*

A much sought after heart specialist performed a major heart surgery on a patient. While performing the surgery he lost something and killed the patient. He lost his memory.

*

Absent minded doctor: "This medicine is for your headache."

Patient: "I don't have a headache and don't wish to have one taking this medicine?"

*

If a patient is poor, the doctor will cure him fast. If a patient is rich, the doctor will prolong his curing process.

*

A doctor before leaving for a two-week vacation abroad entrusted his practice to his son, a young doctor. When the doctor returned from his vacation, his son briefed him on what he had done for the two weeks. He also mentioned to his father that he had successfully cured five of his patients who had been seeing him for many years. The father said, "Well son, you have in fact done a very good job. But the five wealthy patients you cured were the ones who enabled me to see you through your medical studies. I now have to look for another five wealthy patients to see your sister through her law studies." The surprised son said, "Dad, I never ever realized that there was so much to learn in this profession."

*

Patient: "Doctor, I keep forgetting things?"
Doctor: "When did you first realize that?"
Patient: "When did I first realize what?"

*

A heart surgeon's wife should not let her husband know that the way to a man's heart is through his stomach!

*

A doctor was using his stethoscope but was unable to feel the patient's heart beat. Surprised, the doctor looked at the patient. The patient said, "I have dextrocardia." Asked the doctor, "What in the whole white world is that?" The patient replied, "I have my heart on the right side." The doctor trying to hide his embarrassment said, "Oh, I see," and continued examining the patient.

*

A visitor to a hospital noticed several nurses wearing badges designed like an apple. The curious visitor asked one of the nurses if it signified something. The nurse replied, "No, it's just to keep the doctors away."

*

Nurse Evelyn: "Apples don't work with one particular doctor."
Nurse Monica: "Which doctor?"
Nurse Evelyn: "Dr. Adam."

*

Nurse: "Doctor, the patient you just treated collapsed at the entrance."
Doctor: "Quick, go and turn him to the other direction, so he'll appear to have just arrived."

*

Patient: "Doctor, you've got to help me. I just can't stop my hands from shaking."
Doctor: "Do you drink a lot?"
Patient: "Not really. I spill most of it."

*

Patient: "Doctor, I have this nagging pain in my right leg."
Doctor: "That's because of old age."
Patient: "But my left leg is of the same age and there is nothing wrong with it."
Doctor: "Looks like you have another problem now. Your left leg is not catching up with your age."

*

A Kleptomaniac was cured of his ailment by his doctor. When he visited his doctor a month later, he told the doctor, "I'm very grateful to you for curing me. I wonder how I'm going to repay you."
Doctor: "Repay me? Well, if ever you got into a relapse, I'd love to have a brand new 32" television."

*

Doctor: "I'm afraid I have some very bad news for you. You're dying and you don't have much time left."
Patient: "Oh, that's terrible. How long have I got?"
Doctor: "Ten."
Patient: "Ten? Ten what? Months, weeks, days, what?"
Doctor: "Nine."

*

Do doctors sleep with their patients?
Some do.
How about veterinarians?
Some do.

*

A doctor received a call in the middle of the night from a man who said, "Doctor, my mother-in-law is dying. Can you come immediately and pull her through?"

*

Doctor: "Was there any insanity in your family?"
Patient: "Yes, my late father was insane right up to his last breath. He thought he was the boss of the house."

*

Two hours after performing a successful heart transplant operation, the doctor rushed to the operating theatre and was frantically searching for his wedding ring. Seeing this, one of the nurses whispered into the ear of another nurse, "I think it's inside the patient." The other nurse whispered back, "Poor guy has to undergo another operation and I wonder what kind of a lie the doctor is going to tell him."

*

A doctor returned home in the wee hours of the morning. His surprised wife asked him, "How come you look happy and not tired?" The doctor replied, "I attended to four house calls and luckily all the patients were living near by. I'm happy because I killed four birds with one stone."

*

Patient: "I'm so frightened, this is my first operation."
Doctor: "I truly can understand how you feel. It's my first operation too."

*

A doctor after a two week hunting trip returned home and complained to his wife. He said, "I was there for two weeks but I didn't kill a damn thing!" Trying to console him, the wife said, "Well darling, that's what you get for neglecting your practice."

*

A doctor told a patient who was about to under-go an operation, "This is a very delicate operation and only one in five survives. Do you have anything to say?" "Yes," said the patient, "Please help me put on my shirt and pants."

*

A doctor received a call in the middle of the night. The voice said, "Doctor, I can't sleep. Can you help me?" The doctor replied, "I'm feeling very sleepy. Please call someone else to sing you a lullaby."

*

Doctor: "How are you now, Mr. Brown, after your heart operation?"
Mr. Brown: "Well doctor, it's strange that I now have two heart beats."
The doctor's face turned pale and he spoke to himself, "Oh dear, now I know where my wrist-watch is!"

*

Patient: "Doctor, I'm so depressed, I feel like killing myself. What shall I do?"
Doctor: "Leave that to me."

*

Doctor: "You are suffering from a severe depression. I'll prescribe some medicine for you. On your part you should learn how to be cheerful and don't take your troubles and worries to bed."
Patient: "But doctor, my wife won't sleep alone."

*

Doctor to patient: "How are you?"
Patient: "I, in fact, came to find that out from you."

*

A worried husband phoned the doctor at two in the morning and said, "Doctor, please rush to my house, my wife has appendicitis."
Doctor: "Stop being ridiculous. Four years ago I operated on her for appendicitis. Have you ever heard of a second appendix?"
The husband asked, "Ever heard of a second wife!"

*

Samson called the doctor's office and told the receptionist he needed to see the doctor immediately. The receptionist said, "I'm sorry the doctor is fully booked for two weeks. I can only arrange an appointment for you two weeks from now."
Samson: "But I could be dead by then!"
Receptionist: "No problem. So long as your wife or any of your relatives inform us, we'll cancel the appointment."

*

Patient: "Doctor, I'm walking in my sleep. Is there anyway you could cure it?"
Doctor: "Yes certainly. Here are four boxes of thump tags. Before you go to bed fill your bedroom floor with these thump tags."

*

Patient: "Nurse, I'm at death's door."
Nurse: "Don't worry, the doctor will pull you through."

*

17

Lawyers

Smith: "How do you find the lawyer I recommended you?"
James: "Well, I don't think I'm going to engage him as my lawyer."
Smith: "Do you know he is one of the leading lawyers in town?"
James: "He may be and I don't care. It irked me when he told me that he was an honest lawyer. How could he be so blatantly dishonest about his honesty!"

*

You are trapped in a room with a stray dog, a nasty cat and a lawyer. You have a gun with two bullets. What would you do?
I'll shoot the lawyer twice.

*

A lawyer was walking along the street and there was an accident. He rushed to the spot, handed his name cards to both the drivers and said, "I saw the whole thing, I'll take either side."

*

Lawyer: "Doctor, I have noticed that you always ask your patients what they had for dinner."
Doctor: "It's a form of evaluation. How else would I know how much to charge them."
Lawyer: "It's high time I started asking my clients which posh restaurants they dine."

*

Daughter to father: "My boy friend drives two expensive cars, he lives in a rich neighbourhood, he has a lot of money in the bank and he is much sought after by the rich and famous."

Father: "Is your boy friend a lawyer?"

Daughter: "Oh dad, how did you know that?"

Father: "From all the lies he had told you."

Daughter: "But I'm in love daddy and want to marry him."

Father: "You certainly can marry him because something tells me this young man will one day become a prominent lawyer. He appears to be a better liar than most of the other lawyers."

*

Prosecution lawyer to defence lawyer: "You are a dirty old scoundrel!"

Defence lawyer: "You are a cheat and a liar!"

Judge: "Let the case proceed, now that the learned counsels have indentified each other."

*

Singapore

A shoe shop at Lucky Plaza in Singapore has this sign placed outside the shop: "Buy one and get one free." (Looks like this is the only shoe shop in the world which doesn't sell foot wears in pairs).

*

In the public buses and trains in Singapore some people seated keep their eyes closed and pretend to be sleeping because they hate to see old people or pregnant women standing nearby.

*

Hokkien is a Chinese dialect widely spoken in Singapore and Malaysia. "Ah Siow" in Hokkien means mad man or mad person. The official lunatic asylum in Singapore is called the Institute of Mental Health. The receptionist at the Institute of Mental Health received a call. The caller asked, "Can I speak to Mr. Ah Siow, please?" The receptionist giggled then asked, "All of them here are Ah Siows. Which Ah Siow do you wish to speak to?" The caller replied, "Mr. Tan Ah Siow." The receptionist went through the register then told the caller, "There are 28 Tan Ah Siows, which one?"

*

Malaysia

In Malaysia, no one believed the politician sodomised his assistant until he made an official denial.

*

Myanmar

Since the supporters of Aung San Suu Kyi in Myanmar were unable to openly support her because of the military junta, they migrated to other countries to support themselves.

*

Australia

An Australian tour guide asked a tourist, "Did you come here to-die?" Replied the tourist, "Look, I didn't come here to die. I came here to visit your country and return home alive and that too in one piece!"

*

Marriage - Part I

If a young woman married an old man, she did it because she was deeply in love with his money. If a young man marries an old woman it simply means that this young man is penniless, homeless, jobless, senseless and above all tasteless.

*

Sam: "Barking dogs seldom bite."
John: "I know of a dog which barks and scratches your face."
Sam: "Really!"
John: "Yes and incidentally I'm married to that dog."

*

Love is blind and marriage is a union between two temporarily blinded stooges.

*

Marriages are made in heaven and transferred to hell three months to a year after honeymoon. The period of transformation from angels to devils differ from woman to woman.

*

They say in marriage better the known devil than the unknown. I'm puzzled. What difference does that make any way?
(Among some tribes in Africa, a man doesn't know his wife until he marries her. In all the other parts of the world, most men strongly believe that they know the women they are going to marry "inside out" until they get married. After marriage it will gradually dawn on them that whether a known devil or an unknown one doesn't really make a difference).

*

John is a very brave man. He is not afraid of devils because he lives with one.

*

In the first year of marriage, the man speaks and the woman listens. In the second year, the woman speaks and the man listens. In the third year, they both speak and the neighbours listen. In the fourth year, their lawyers speak and the judge listens. In the fifth year, the mother speaks and the son listens, "I told you not to marry that bitch. You never listened. You were madly in love with her then. See, what has happened to you now. ....!"

*

She was on her knees begging her husband who was hiding under the bed to come out and fight like a man.

*

This is truly an inseparable young couple. It took 8 police personnel and 4 passers-by to separate them outside their house.

*

A wife, during a quarrel blasted, "I am a fool to marry you." Replied the husband, "How nice if you had told me the truth about yourself before I married you. That would have saved me from becoming another 'you'!"

*

John despises the alarm clock more than his wife. It irritates him especially when he's having a very deep sleep and has extreme difficulty waking up. His wife is less sinful, she only irritates him when he's wide awake.

*

Wives usually don't admit their mistakes; instead they justify their mistakes and on most occasions they go the extra mile to put the blame squarely on the 'poor thing' called "**husband**".

*

A musician is going to marry a dancer. He certainly is a lucky guy because it's rare for a husband to make his wife dance to his tune.

*

Nancy to Shirley: "I heard your mother-in-law slipped and fell down. You were standing near by but did not bother to carry her up."

Shirley: "I didn't carry her up on my doctor's advice."

Nancy: "On your doctor's advice?"

Shirley: "Yes, my doctor advised me not to carry heavy things."

*

Sheila: "You met my parents yesterday. What did they say?"

Suresh: "Sheila, I don't think we can get married."

Sheila: "Why, did my parents say something?"

Suresh: "No, I met your younger sister."

*

A Middle-Aged Bachelor: "I regret not getting married."

A Middle-Aged Married Man: "I regret getting married."

A Middle-Aged Divorcee: "I regret getting married and now I don't regret not getting remarried."

*

"Do you say your prayers before you eat?"

"Only on those occasions when I'm forced to eat my wife's cooking."

*

There are two types of women. The one you dream of getting married to and the one you marry.

*

I'm married and I can't ask for a better wife. I'd love to but I can't.

*

However hard they crack their heads or tear their hair, men just can't understand women. They are such a mystery. Yet they get married and end up in misery.

*

What's the difference between a wise man and one who is naïve?
A wise man dates as many girls as possible and doesn't get married to any.
A naïve man falls in love at first sight and gets married.

*

You get married. Then your friend gets married. Once you see what he has, you tell yourself, "How nice if I had his."

*

Wife: "Darling if I die, will you remarry?"
Husband: "I'm still young now. But if it happens 30 years later how the heck am I going to remarry? You must be fair to me."

*

Wife: "Honey if I die, will you marry again?"
Husband: "Well, if I say yes, you will be angry and if I say no, you know I am lying."

*

In sports you can aim for the gold medal. But in marriage be contended with a silver. When making love, let your wife come first and you come a close second.

*

Wife: "I'm coming; I'm coming, faster, faster. I'm coming, I'm coming, faster, faster." The car came to a screeching halt at the petrol kiosk and the husband said, "Quick, rush to the toilet and get your business done."

*

Men are born free and equal. Some men remain that way others get married.

*

Are all men fools? It's not true. Some are bachelors.

*

Jane: "I want to introduce Doris to my husband."
Jessie: "You hate her like poison, then why introduce her to your husband?"
Jane: "I've suffered enough with him for 10 years. I want her to have an affair with him, marry him and suffer more than what I'm suffering now."
Jessie: "Has your husband ever mentioned to you about his ex-wife?"
Jane: "No, I don't even know her name."
Jessie: "It is Doris and she had already done what you just said to you 10 years ago!"

*

60% of married Singaporean men cheat in Singapore, the rest cheat in Batam, Balai, Tanjong Pinang and Bangkok. The rich Singaporean men cheat in America, Europe, Australia and in the Middle East when traveling alone. Rumour mongers say that some middle aged married women during their business trips abroad engage the services of gigolos.

*

A 98 year old man married an 18 year old virgin. On the first night of their honeymoon both of them were sitting on the bed and crying because she didn't know what to do and he had forgotten what to do.

*

A happy marriage is a matter of give and take; the husband gives and the wife takes. Before marriage a man had the freedom and luxury to laugh all the way to the bank. After marriage he sorrowfully deposits with a slight nagging pain in the heart and the wife laughs and giggles all the way to the bank.

*

Nephew: "Uncle I'm planning to get married. Can you give me a rough estimate as to how much it will cost me?"
Uncle: "Your wedding may not cost you much but your marriage will."
Nephew: "How much will a marriage costs?"
Uncle: "I've been married for over 30 years now and am still paying for it."

*

Two friends, John and Smith, who had not met each other for a long time were engrossed in an interesting conversation and in the course of their conversation John enquired about Smith's wife.

Smith: "She's an angel."

John: "You are lucky. Mine is still alive."

*

Two friends were enjoying their drinks in a bar. One asked the other, "Do you ever speak to your wife when making love?"

His friend replied, "There were several occasions when she called me on my hand phone. I'll tell her, darling I'm very busy now and call her back after I'm done."

*

What's the difference between knowledge and faith?

A wife with four children knows who fathered her children - that's **knowledge**.

The husband believes all the four children are his - that's **faith**.

*

They say spare the rod and spoil the child. In marriage if you spare the rod someone else will make your wife pregnant.

*

The utter frustration of being the best man in a wedding is that you don't get a chance to prove it.

*

Husband: "Darling, our maid is very stubborn and defiant. I don't think you'll be able to make her obey you."
Wife: "Nonsense dear. Do you remember how stubborn you were when we first got married?"
Husband: "Well darling, I'm your husband and I didn't have a choice but the maid has. She could choose to leave any moment."

*

Husband and wife were having a very heated argument and the husband shouted, "Shut your stinking gap now before you bring the animal in me out!" The wife retorted, "Who the hell is afraid of a hamster!"

*

Wife: "Why are you home so early?"
Husband: "My boss told me to go to hell."

*

Marriages are made in heaven and dragged down to hell by your wife and mother-in-law.

*

Marriages are made in heaven. So are thunder and lightning.

*

A young priest who just got married told his wife, "Darling, I'm going to pray for guidance." His wife replied, "Sweetheart, I'll take care of your guidance. You pray for your endurance."

*

A very timid and obedient husband couldn't take his wife's bullying anymore. So he decided to consult a psychiatrist. The psychiatrist said, "You are a man, behave like a real man and show her you are the boss. The newly inspired and rejuvenated husband returns home and mustering enough courage tells his wife, "Look here lady, from now on I'm the boss of the house and your job is to obediently carry out my orders. Now, serve my dinner right away after which go upstairs and lay out my pants and shirt, I'm going out with my friends and you are going to stay at home where you belong. One more thing, do you know who's going to comb my hair, button my shirt and wear my tie?" "I certainly do," says the wife calmly, "The undertaker!"

*

Jason to John: "John, Smith just got married and he looks happy. I could understand that. But you have been married for over ten years. You look happier than Smith. I couldn't understand that."
John: "Well Jason, my wife has finally agreed to a divorce and I'm now seeing my newly found girl friend, my new secretary."

*

What do married men do immediately after sex? Some fall asleep, some go to the bathroom to wash up, some roll over and light up a cigarette and the rest, almost 60%, get dressed and go home.

*

Morris went to see his boss in his office and told him, "Boss, I have a lot of household chores to do. I need to paint my house, clean up the whole house and mow the lawn. Can I take off on Thursday?"

Boss: "Morris, you know we are short-handed and how can I let you take off on Thursday."

Morris: "Thanks boss, I knew I could count on you," and added, "Do me a favour boss. I'll call my wife and you explain to her."

*

Wife: "Darling, could you please change the bulbs in the living room."

Husband: "Am I an electrician?"

The next day she approaches her husband again and says, "Dear, can you please fix the kitchen tap, it's leaking."

Husband: "Am I a plumber?"

The following day on returning home from work, he finds everything fixed. He asks his wife, "Who fixed it?" She replies, "A very helpful friend of mine." Curious, the husband asks, "Did he ask for anything?" "Yes dear," says the wife, "He asked me to either bake a cake for him or go to bed with him."

Husband: "So you baked him a cake."

Wife: "Am I a baker?"

*

A guy who has been frequenting the brothels for years finally married a whore unaware that she was previously involved in the world's oldest profession. On their honeymoon trip, after making love to her for the first time, the guy absent-mindedly gave her $40. She took the money and returned him $20.

*

In a bachelor's life troubles came and go. In a married man's life troubles come and hardly go. They stay put especially in bed.

*

A wife gave birth to a son and the husband rushed to the hospital. He saw the baby and was shocked. Horrified, he asked his wife, "We have three beautiful daughters but this baby boy is so ugly. Have you been cheating on me?" Wife: "Not this time, dear."

*

A man is incomplete until he is married. Then he is finished. A bachelor is also incomplete but is never finished. He keeps on dating different girls till there is no end to it.

*

A bachelor is free to choose and chooses to be free.

*

Do smart men make better husbands?
No, smart men don't get married.

*

Miscellaneous – Part 1

Jason, on his death bed confessed to Alfred, "Alfred, I feel very guilty for doing a lot of bad things to you."
Alfred: "What do you mean?"
Jason: "You see Alfred, I had an affair for a long time with your wife, I made your wife sell your sports car and pocketed the money, I forged several of your cheques and drew money out of your bank account, stole your costly watch and killed your dog."
Alfred: "Since you have confessed, I'm beginning to feel guilty."
Jason: "But why?"
Alfred: "I'm the one who poisoned you."

*

Joyce: "I heard that your husband had lately been playing golf with George Bearishbull. This guy invites people to play golf with him and sweet talks them into investing their money in some financial instruments promising high returns. But actually the investment is highly speculative and risky. You could lose all your investment. Make sure he doesn't brainwash your husband into investing a large sum of his hard earned money."
Cindy: "Not to worry, it will never happen. How could he wash something my husband doesn't have!"

*

Mama kangaroo to papa kangaroo, crying uncontrollably, "Our baby had been pick-pocketed while I was asleep."

*

Two thieves saw the police approaching them at the 14th floor of a building. They had no choice but to jump down. The professional thieves carefully jumped down and each landed on a pedestrian killing both the pedestrians and the two thieves escaped unhurt. (That's what you call a miraculous escape with a professional touch).

*

A miser won the lottery yet he put on a long face. When asked why, he said, "I feel very dejected for wasting a dollar on the second ticket."

*

Norman was showing his holiday pictures to his friend Smith. One of the photos showed him riding a donkey on the beach. "That's a good picture of you," said Smith, "But who's that sitting on your back?"

*

When crossing the road how do you use a zebra crossing? Jump on to its back!

*

Edwin: "I went to the zoo last Sunday."
Charlie: "I was there too."
Edwin: "That's funny. How come I didn't see you in any of the cages?"

*

Some girls go out every Saturday night and sow wild oats then go to the church on Sunday and pray for a crop failure.

*

A very mean lady: "I suppose this horrible picture is what you call modern art?"
Artist: "That's a mirror and what you described as a horrible picture is actually your face."

*

Virginity is like a bubble, once pricked, it's gone forever. Further pricking can cause the stomach to swell.

*

It takes a lot of experience, imagination and practice for a girl to kiss like a beginner.

*

A guy went into a barber shop and asked the barber how long will it take for him to have a haircut. The barber counted the number of customers in his shop and told the guy it would take about two hours. He left but did not return to have his hair cut. He came back after four days and asked the barber the same question. The barber looked around and said, "About two and a half hours." The guy left but did not return for a haircut. This went on once every three or four days. When the eighth time the guy came, asked the same question and left, the curious barber asked his assistant to follow the guy to see where he was going. The assistant return after forty-five minutes. The barber asked his assistant, "Where did he go? The assistant replied, "To your house."
(**Expert Opinion -** Despite repeated assurances from the barber's wife, this guy, being a very careful person just wanted to be "doubly sure").

*

A famous philosopher once said, "If you hear no evil, see no evil, speak no evil and do no evil, then you are a born wasted."

*

What do a gynecologist and a pizza delivery boy have in common?
They can both smell it but can't eat it.

*

Husband: "Why are you not playing cards with Betty anymore?"
Wife: "Would you play cards with someone who keeps cheating?"
Husband: "Of course not!"
Wife: "Neither would Betty."

*

Be nice to your kids because they are the ones who'll be choosing your nursing home.

*

Joseph: "Grace, will you marry me?"
Grace: "No, but I truly appreciate your good taste."

*

Peter: "Lucy, will you marry me?"
Lucy: "If we got married I certainly would appreciate your good taste. But my family, relatives and friends will despise me and shun me for my bad taste."

*

Two mountain climbers reached the top of Mount Everest. Though exhausted, they screamed out of joy and hugged each other.

First Mountain Climber: "This is a life time achievement. I'm so happy. Bring out our national flag; let's plant it right here."

Second Mountain Climber: "I thought you brought it."

*

Rodney was walking with a duck under his arm in a small town. His friend, Harold who was passing by stopped and asked, "What are you doing with that pig?" Taken aback, Rodney asked, "Can't you see, this is a duck and not a pig!" Replied Harold, "I wasn't talking to you Rodney. I was talking to the duck."

*

A delivery man was struggling with a large package. A passer-by offered to help. They both grabbed an end and began to struggle with the package. After fifteen minutes they were both exhausted. Said the delivery man, "I give up. We are never going to get the package on the truck." "On to the truck," asked the passer-by, "I thought you were trying to get it off the truck."

*

A lady visiting an orchard was amazed with the variety and abundance of fruits grown in the trees. She asked the farmer, "What do you do with all these fruits?" The farmer replied, "We eat what we can and what we can't, we can.

*

A city dweller went to a farm and bought a beautiful horse. The farmer explained, "This is a special kind of horse. He'll only move if you say, "Praise the Lord". "To stop him, you have to say "Amen"." The city dweller got on to the horse and yelled, "Praise the Lord," and the horse took off with great speed. Soon the horse and rider were heading towards a cliff. Just in time the rider remembered to say "Amen". The horse came to a screeching halt right at the edge of the cliff. Relieved, the rider raised his eyes to heaven and said, "Praise the Lord".

*

A sparrow saw a snail by the side of the road, flew near to the snail and asked the snail where it was going. The snail said, "I am going to New York." The sparrow laughed and said, "Are you crazy, it's now winter in New York and you'll freeze to death!" The snail replied, "Don't worry, it will be summer by the time I reach there."

*

Why do drunken men whistle in the toilet?
So they know which end to wipe.

*

How do porcupines make love?
Carefully, very carefully.

*

A guy who eats beef and mutton insists that he is a vegetarian. According to him cows, goats and sheep are vegetarians. They only eat grass.

*

Whenever his friends narrate a sombre, gloomy or a very sad story, Kenny has the habit of saying, "It could have been worse," which irritates his friends. So they made up a story which they believed Kenny would not have the slightest chance of repeating his "irritating phrase". Meeting at the club bar, one of them said, "Kenny, do you know what happened to Nelson? When he returned home last night, he saw his wife in bed with another man. He shot both of them, then shot himself." "Terrible" said Kenny and added, "But it could have been worse." His friends almost blew their tops. Kenny calmed them down and then explained, "Well, if it had happened the night before, I'd be dead now."

*

For which job are gays much sought after?
Blow job.

*

What do two gays do in bed?
They first get very engrossed in performing the 69, then they are passionately engaged in caressing and penetrating each other's posterior.

*

When a reporter asked a famous singer why he broke up with his long time, live-in gay partner, the singer replied, "I don't like people doing things behind my back!"

*

What is Premature Ejaculation?
Something you get faster than you expected and in the process frustrate your "sleeping partner".

*

A businessman doesn't go to bed with them yet they are called his sleeping partners. A more appropriate term would be non-active business associates or partners.

*

Do you need to be trained to become a rubbish collector?
Not necessarily. You'll be able to pick it up as you go along.

*

Who is an idiot?
One who can't swim and tests the depth of water with both legs.

*

In a hundred meters sprint event what does the "record breaking winner" lose?
His breath.

*

We were born naked, wet and hungry. Then things got worse.

*

The poor thing called "The Leaning Tower of Pisa" has had the inclination for a long, long time but none of the visitors including humans, dogs, cats, mice and not to mention donkeys was turned on or had the urge to satiate it's craving (lust).

*

A robber was running with a lot of money stashed in his bag. Two cops gave chase and caught him. The robber told the cops, "I'm rushing to save a patient's life. She's my mother who'll be undergoing a complicated operation and the doctors want me to pay in advance." The cops let him go and on reaching their police vehicle it struck one of the cops who exclaimed, "Oh my, he stole the money!" The other cop exclaimed, "Oh my, he didn't only steal the money, he told us a big fat lie!"

*

While travelling on a bridge one of the car tyres burst. The man stopped his car and changed the tyre. While changing, the four screws rolled and fell into the river. The driver didn't know what to do. Just then a guy standing behind a huge fence called and told the driver to take one screw each from the other three tyres and use them on the fourth tyre. He then told the driver to drive slowly to the nearest service station which was about a kilometer away. After fixing the tyre he turned to thank the guy and saw a sign on the top of the fence which read, "Lunatic Asylum'. Surprised, the driver asked, "Are you mad?" Replied the guy loudly, "I may be mad but I'm not as stupid as you are!"

*

An irritated customer in a bar who was not allowed to smoke at his table snapped at the bartender, "Isn't making a smoking section in a bar like making a peeing section in a swimming pool!"

*

A guy dated a not so pretty girl and took her to his house. Once inside his bedroom he asked her to close the door and lock it. She did. He then asked her to sit on the bed. She did. He then asked her to lie down on the bed. She did. He then asked her to take off her clothes. She did. Then he told her, "April fool."

*

An Indian proverb says, "If you fondle your dog too much it will embarrass you by licking you in all the wrong places in a public place."

*

First Mother: "My son is seventeen years old. He smokes, drinks, keeps late nights and argues with me and his father. Do you have a son who behaves like mine?'
Second Mother: "My son doesn't smoke, drink, keep late nights or argue."
First Mother: "Oh my, such a wonderful son. How old is he?"
Second Mother: "Two years old."

*

He made his money manufacturing trousers and lost it on skirts.

*

An overjoyed politician called his wife and said, "I've been elected."

Wife: "Honestly?"

Politician: "Now, why go into that."

*

Why are hurricanes usually named after women?
When they come, they are wild and wet, but when they go, they take your house and car with them.

*

Two of them are walking along a busy street. One of them is the father of the other person's son. What is their relationship?
Husband and wife.

*

Two of them are walking along a dimly lighted back alley. One of them is the father of the other person's daughter. What is their relationship?
Another man's wife and her illicit lover.

*

Security Guards

Security guards wear uniform to identify themselves. This enables others to know who the bloke is, sleeping inside the guard post.

*

Who could dose off while standing. Security guards with no less than five years experience. The art of standing and dosing off can't be mastered overnight, it takes years!

*

If a security guard is caught sleeping in a chair, he'll swear he wasn't sleeping and insist that he was just resting his eyes.

*

Does a security guard wearing a tie and standing under the sun look smart to anyone? To me he looks like a clown for no fault of his. He's forced to wear such an attire by his boss or he doesn't get paid.

*

Why does a retired Regional Marketing Manager (once a high flier) work as a security officer? To escape from all the household chores; from his nagging wife who's suffering from post menu-pause blues and from babysitting his grandchildren.

*

Work hard or work smart. How to work hard when you are lazy and how to work smart when you are stupid. Don't lose hope, there is still light at the end of the tunnel. Become a security guard!

*

He is a very alert security officer. Even the slightest noise could wake him up.

*

Police Officer

Police officers wear their uniform for self protection. Robbers won't dare rob them. But if a police officer is not wearing his uniform on his off day and a robber points a gun at him chances are he'll shit in his pants.

*

Preacher, Priest or Father?

A preacher enjoys preaching very much because he doesn't have to practise what he preaches. It's meant for those listening to his sermon and he is very particular they faithfully practise what he preaches.

*

A preacher is the only one capable of keeping over a hundred wives' mouths shut, all at the same time, for an hour or two.

*

Why do they call a priest 'Father' when he is neither married nor fathered any children?

*

Preacher to car mechanic: "Please don't charge me very high for the repair. You know I'm a poor preacher."
Mechanic: "Yes, I do. I heard your sermon last Sunday. It's amazing you can put quite a lot of them to sleep all at the same time!"

*

Priest, visiting Adolf in hospital said, "Now Adolf, I shall pray for you to forgive Raymond for hitting you with a metal rod."

Adolf: "Don't bother Father, wait till I'm out of here and then you can pray for Raymond."

*

Young Priest: "He has confessed to stealing a crate of whisky. What shall I tell him?"

Old Priest: "Tell him we don't pay more than two dollars a bottle."

*

Father James and father Joseph sneaked into a bar. They noticed, to their disappointment, there wasn't a single girl in the bar. It then struck them that they were in a gay bar. Just then a man came, sat beside father Joseph and started caressing him. Father Joseph was dumbfounded. Father James then went near the man and whispered something into his ear. The man nodded his head and walked away. Relieved, father Joseph thanked father James and asked, "What did you tell him?" Father James said, "I told him we're on our honeymoon."

*

During a Sunday service in a church, the priest said, "You all know you can't take it with you when you 'leave', so place as much as you can on the collection plate."

*

A Birthday Greeting

Happy Birthday to you and many more happy returns of the day.
I wish you the very best with all my heart, throat, lungs, rib cage and intestines (small as well as large).

*

What is an alarm clock?

It is a small, handy mechanical device to wake up lazy people who have no children and never bothered to have any.

*

Jason has broken several alarm clocks for disturbing his sleep.

*

An alarm clock is a small handy mechanical device which disturbs your deep heavenly sleep and tells you, "Wake up you idiot and start facing hell again!"

*

Water

We can go without food for days but not without water. Water is indispensable for almost all living things. But the same water has killed more people than deadly diseases, missiles, bombs, earthquakes, fire and poison. Beware of water!

*

Milk

"Is this milk fresh?"
"Fresh? Three hours ago it was grass."

*

Mum's Cooking

Nothing like mum's cooking. Since day one most of us have been eating the junk food our mummy cooks and have unknowingly developed a taste for it. So certainly, nothing like mum's cooking!

*

Mother Tongue

Mothers do the tongue lashing almost all the time and fathers remain as passive listeners. That's why a language is called the mother tongue.

*

Fishes

If fishes are not greedy of worms and could keep their mouths shut, they won't be caught and eaten by Man. But if they keep their mouths shut, they can't take in oxygen and can be dead in no time.
Solution - They must not be greedy of worms, keep their mouths open and lie low. They can keep their mouths wide open near the surface of the water on rainy days. Besides, they can visit the outside world during a tsunami

and return with the return waves. If they missed the return wave just like many missing the flight, they can always flip flop back to the sea and live happily ever after.

*

We wash the fish before we cook. That's a terrible insult to a fish which has lived in water all its life.

*

A fish in a fish market, still alive, sighs, "If only I had kept my mouth shut, I wouldn't be here now."

*

Which is the most valuable fish?
The Goldfish.

*

Which is the most adorable fish?
The Angelfish.

*

What fish makes a good pudding?
Jellyfish.

*

Which fish goes to heaven when it dies?
Angelfish.

*

What do you call a fish that only cares about itself?
Shellfish.

*

Weatherman

A weatherman insists that he doesn't lie, but is clueless as to why his weather forecast is almost all the time wrong.

*

A weatherman dislikes being compared to a lawyer, fortune teller and a politician. He laments, "They all tell lies and make money. I don't."

*

A weatherman is one who forecasts the weather almost all the time incorrectly and if queried puts the blame squarely on the unpredictable weather.

*

A weatherman is protected by the law. He cannot be implicated for persistently forecasting the weather wrongly.

*

Most people wonder if the weathermen are using very effective instruments/equipment to forecast the weather or they let these instruments/equipment collect dust and toss coins:- heads – rain, tails - sunshine, heads – thunder storm, tails -heat wave, heads -tsunami, tails - cyclone!!!

*

An old man has a rope hanging from a pole in his garden and he claims the rope forecasts the weather better than a weather forecast department. When it moves it's windy;

when it's wet it's a rainy day; when it's dry it's a sunny day and if the pole and rope swing violently, a cyclone is approaching.

*

Professional Wrestlers

It looks like professional wrestlers rehearse several days before the actual match. If not how could they fake so naturally? How about referees and commentators? They need only to rehearse one day before the match.

*

Boxing

Boxer complaining to his coach, "Isn't it a long way from the changing room to the ring?" His opponent walking behind overheard and snapped, "Don't worry you won't have to walk back to the changing room after the bout!"

*

Jockeys

Jockeys are those pint-sized stooges who take thousands of punters for a ride, all at the same time, on a race track.

*

Economist

An economist is an expert who confidently predicts what will happen and when it doesn't happen, explains in detail with several economic jargons why it didn't happen.

*

Prime Minister

A reporter asked an 85 years old Prime Minister who has been holding the position for 50 years, "Mr. Prime Minister, when was the last time you had an erection?"
Prime Minister: "You mean election? This morning just before blekfast."
Reporter: "Even at this age you are still in fighting spirit. I'm impressed. May I know your secret, sir?"
Prime Minister: "Viagla."

*

Hermaphrodite or she-male

Hermaphrodite or she-male is an adorably beautiful and sexy person with a tight penetrative posterior. Has beautiful kissable lips and a mouth which serves as a suction pump much to the delight and satisfaction of most men both married and unmarried.

*

Cross-Eyed Judge

Three men were in the dock and the crossed-eyed judge said to the first: "How do you plead?"
"Not guilty." said the second.
"I'm not talking to you." snapped the judge.
"I didn't say a word." said the third.

*

Interview

Interviewer: "You are here for a job interview, why are you taking off your clothes?"
Female interviewee: "Oh dear, I'm terribly sorry. You looked like my gynaecologist. For a moment I thought I was in his clinic."

*

Consultant

A consultant is one who knows a hundred ways of making love but is still a virgin.

*

Lipstick

Why is something which can't stick a woman's lips together disallowing them to nag, brag or gossip called a lipstick?

*

A Very Scary Experience

Jason: "My granny once had a very scary experience. She faced a ferocious lion approaching her menacingly. She was scared to death but managed to put up a brave front and stared at the lion. The lion came close to my granny and roared."
George: "Oh my, what happened then?"
Jason: "My granny couldn't take it anymore and quickly walked away from the cage."

*

Vasectomy

What do Christmas trees and vasectomised men have in common?
They both have balls for decoration.

*

What is vasectomy?
Vasectomy is an operation performed on men to transform the balls into a decoration item.

*

Who is a nun?

A nun is one who covers from top to toe and conceals her feelings in public and gets extremely wild in private with either her male or female counterpart.

*

Insanity

Researchers have discovered that a mad person doesn't actually suffer from insanity. He enjoys every moment of it. He remains a happy person and makes those sane people around him suffer by driving them crazy.

*

Hiccup

A guy with a hiccup knocked at a door and asked for a glass of water. The man went in and came out with a gun and pointed it at him. The guy was shocked. Then the man asked, "Has your hiccup stopped?"

*

Marriage – Part 2

What is the difference between a bachelor and a married man?
A bachelor has half a brain and a married man has no brains.

*

Why do men want to marry virgins?
To avoid criticism.

*

Honeymoon
A job orientation a man has to undergo before beginning to work under a new boss.

*

After twenty years of marriage the husband prefers a quickie but his wife still prefers it slow, gentle and longer than ever before.

*

Women are luckier than men. They can fake orgasm, men can't.

*

What frustrates a woman most?
Her husband's early withdrawal.

*

Adam came first, but then, most men always do and in the process frustrate their "sleeping partners".

*

Noticing his wife having bought a new puppy, the husband asked her sarcastically, "You are already treating me like a dog, why do you need another one?"
Wife: "Look you are my husband and this is my pet."
Husband: "Well then, why don't you give my name to your pet."
Wife: "That would be an insult to the puppy."
Husband: "Never mind my name but just out of curiosity, are you hesitant to give your name to the puppy fearing it might commit suicide out of disgrace."

*

They say there's always a woman behind a man's success, then who's the woman behind a man's misery, frustration, irritation, depression and down fall?

*

A couple decided to divorce after 50 years of marriage. They have been seeing too much of each other for too long and simply could not stand the sight of each other especially in the nude.

*

Peter never believed in Hell until he married his wife, Mrs. Peter.

*

If you are so depressed and decided to commit suicide; would you hang yourself, jump down from a tall building or take poison?

I wouldn't bother doing any of those things. If I decided to commit suicide all I need to do is to eat my wife's cooking.

*

Divorce is a Latin word which means hit a man hard where it hurts him most. His genital? No his pocket!

*

Advice to husbands - You can argue with your wife but make sure she wins the argument or else your life is going to get even more miserable than what it already is now.

*

Wife: "Are you listening to me?"
Husband: "I certainly am. Can't you see me yawning?"

*

Samuel: "Darling, if we got married do you think you could live on my income?"
Joan: "I certainly can but what will you live on?" After a pause, Joan said, "I have an idea. You take up a second job."

*

Ivan: "I got married because I was sick and tired of eating out, washing my laundry, ironing my clothes, tidying up the house, watering the plants and mowing the lawn."
Alex: "That's funny. I divorced for the same reasons."

*

Grace: "My husband has the habit of beating me every morning."
Sharon: "That's terrible."
Grace: "He always wakes up an hour earlier than I do."

*

On bed
Husband: "Honey, you're dry tonight."
Wife: "You are licking the bed sheet, dear"

*

A man will pay $2 for a $1 item he needs.
A woman will pay $1 for a $2 item she doesn't need.

*

A woman marries a man expecting he will change, but he doesn't.
A man marries a woman expecting she won't change, but she does

*

When a man runs away with your wife, there is no better punishment (revenge) than to let him keep her and suffer.

*

Husband - One who is controlled by his wife.
Wife - One who is beyond the control of her husband.

*

If a wife wants equal rights, she has to return some of hers to her husband so that both could be on par.

*

A robber demands your life or your money. A wife demands both.

*

Wife: "Darling, we'll soon be three."
Husband: "Oh my, I'm spellbound. Why didn't you tell me earlier?"
Wife: "My mother only called me this morning and said she'll be here tomorrow."

*

After marriage the curious wife asked her husband, "How many girls have you met?"
He was quiet.
She persisted, "Dear, I'm still waiting."
Husband: "Darling, I'm still counting."

*

William: "I am 60 years old and you know I'm rich. I'm in love with a 20 year old girl. Will she marry me?"
Rodney: "Tell her you are 85 and she will."

*

Wife: "Darling, do you remember my birthday?"
Husband: "I keep forgetting because you don't look a day older since we got married."

*

Florence doesn't mind if her husband leaves her so long as he leaves her enough.

*

Let the woman have the last word in an argument. Anything a man says after that is the beginning of a new argument.

*

He bought a book titled, "How to be a boss in your own house". After having eagerly read almost half the book, he realized that the book was written by a bachelor and in frustration threw it away.

*

A husband must muster enough courage to tell his wife who the real boss is in the house. He must be very brave and look straight in her eyes and say, "Look, you are the boss."

*

Husbands are getting smarter these days. They'll put their wives on a high pedestal only when they need her to scrub the ceiling.

*

A married man can afford to forget his mistakes because he will constantly be reminded of them by his "bitter half".

*

After having been married for quite a while, a married man meets his friend and his wife who are newly married. He looks at his friend's wife and tells himself, "What an adorably beautiful lady. How blissful my life would be if I had her as my wife." By the way, do married women have similar cravings? Well if they don't than there won't be such a thing called "extra marital affair".

*

How does a husband like to spend the evening?
Drinking beer and watching TV.

How does a wife like to spend the evening?
Sipping a cocktail and gossiping on the phone.

*

Social psychologists have discovered that the main cause for extra marital affair, domestic violence and divorce is marriage.

*

Before marriage a man gets to eat his favourite food and watch his favourite programmes on TV. After marriage he eats what his wife cooks and with a beer glass in hand watches his wife's favourite programmes on TV.

*

At work a married man may not like his boss but compared to his boss at home he feels he is anytime better and continues to work for him spending more time at work and lesser time at home.

*

"Love Is Blind" and "Love at First Sight" are so contradictory. What exactly is love then? Love is present infatuation and future misery.

*

Simon: "Has your wife gone on a holiday?"
Jason: "Yes, she has gone to Canada to visit her parents. But what makes you ask this question?"
Simon: "Well, besides the old scars I don't see any fresh ones on your face."

*

What is a man's idea of foreplay?
Doing something with his tongue he doesn't quite like doing.

*

When a husband tells his wife, "Darling, I love you." She knows he is lying but doesn't mind. When he says, "Your are beautiful, my love," deep inside she knows it's a blatant lie, even then, she simply can't help but blush.

*

Love is blind but marriage is a total blackout.

*

Before marriage, a man yearns for the woman he loves. After marriage, the **'y'** disappears.

*

If your wife is lost in a supermarket, either strike a conversation with a beautiful girl or open your wallet, she'll find you."

*

The best way to get your husband to do something is to suggest that he is too old to do it. Results could be wonderfully amazing.

*

They say when a man holds a woman's hand before marriage, it's love, after marriage, it's self-defence.

*

Marriage is a serious matter. It's not a joke because the husband never gets to laugh all the way to the bank.

*

A friendly advice to all remaining happy man. If you feel sorry to marry just be sorry and don't marry.

*

If poison is not a controlled item many husbands would be dead by now.

*

If a wife says, "I love you darling" she is up to something. If a husband says, "I love you darling" he is lying.

*

Love tortures! Marriage punishes! Divorce sucks!

*

Married men think alike. They wonder how the other guy is happily married.

*

What is hell?
Get married and you'll know what it is.

*

What is bigamy?
Making the most stupid mistake a second time.

*

Husband (phoning his wife from his office): "I've got two tickets for the ballet."
Wife: "Oh lovely. I'll start getting ready now."
Husband: "No, you start getting ready tomorrow morning. The tickets are for tomorrow night."

*

A lady with a large flowery hat was stopped at the church entrance by the usher. "Are you a friend of the bride?" he asked. Replied the lady, I'm not a friend of the bride and I'll never be one. I'm the bridegroom's mother!"

*

Lady: "I'd like a shirt for my husband."
Sales assistant: "What size, madam?"
Lady: "I'm not sure of his size but I can get both my hands round his neck. Will that be of some help?"

*

Husbands and wives have one thing in common. Both can be trusted when they are nearby each other and can't be trusted when they are far away from each other.

*

A woman has had eighteen husbands. Only one of these eighteen was her own.

*

A husband told his wife that she didn't have the slightest sense of humour. The wife replied, "That's after I married you."

*

All hell broke loose when a newly married man forgot his wife's birthday.

*

A miser remembers his wife's birthday but doesn't buy her a present. He convinces her by saying, "It's really the thought that counts."

*

A husband in his defence says. "How am I expected to remember your birthday when you never look a day older since I married you ten years ago?"

*

Wife: "Darling, do I look 35?"
Husband: "You once did but not now."

*

A note from the new mother-in-law to the new son-in-law: "Congratulations from your mother-in-law. Twenty-one years ago I sent my daughter to bed with a dummy. Tonight, history repeats itself."

*

I wish the newly wedded couple a happy married life and would like to add; please keep all your ups and downs within the confines of your bed.

*

His wife is a very happy person, so the husband hires a private investigator to find out who is or are responsible for her happiness.

*

A wife accused her husband of infidelity. The husband replied, "You are wrong. In fact, I've been faithful to you most of the time."

*

Alfred: "I didn't sleep with my wife before I married her, did you?"
Desmond: "I've not met your wife yet so how would I know."

*

How did the couple celebrate their 25th anniversary? By observing a 25-minute silence and then heaving a sigh of relief that at least 25 years of marriage is over.

*

The husband had no hard feelings and that was reason enough for the wife to get a divorce.

*

Wife: "Your mother has been living with us for ten long years. I really think it's time she moved out and found a place of her own."
Husband: "Can I move out with her, please, please, please?"

*

Husband: "Why can't you make bread like my mother?"
Wife: "I would if you could make dough like your father!"

*

Wife to husband: "Dear, can I give the left over food I cooked to the beggar across the street?"
Husband: "What harm has he done to you?"

*

Husband: "Happy birthday honey. How do feel being 28 for the 10th time?"

*

Husband: "I'm the head of the family!"
Wife: "If you are the head, I'm your neck. I can turn your head whichever direction I want."

*

How to get rid of my mother-in-law?
Pretend to love her more than your wife. That will do the trick.

*

Behind every successful man stands a surprised wife. Behind every successful woman stands a totally drained out and extremely exhausted husband.

*

Husband to maid: "Don't tell madam I brought a girl home. Keep this $50."
Maid: "But sir, madam always gives me $100 when she brings someone home."

*

When I told a joke to my wife she looked at me sternly and said, "I'll stand a jerk but not a joke from the jerk!"

*

Brother to sister: "It's the first time, as far as I know, Dad cracked a joke and mum laughed her heart out."
Sister: "What was the joke?"
Brother: "Dad told mum, "Its high time your mother found another place to live!"

*

William: "How could Jason be admitted to the hospital? I just saw him yesterday evening with one voluptuous and stunningly beautiful woman."
Benjamin: "So did his wife."

*

Husband: "I'm firing the chauffeur. He nearly got me killed twice this week."
Wife: "Oh darling, please give him another chance."

*

Husband: "Darling, there are some left over food on the table. Shall I throw them away now or place them in the fridge and let you throw them away next week?"

*

Why do mothers-in-law irritate their sons-in-law?
Because they are suffering from a severe post menopause disorder and they badly need to vent their frustration on the most vulnerable person.

*

For every mother-in-law living with her son-in-law, there'll be an irritated neighbour who will want the mother-in-law's bedroom curtain to be kept closed all the time.

*

Why do mothers-in-law pick on their sons-in-law?
Because they are frustrated they don't have their husbands to pick on who left them long ago either dead or alive.

*

Restaurant

The restaurant provides very bad service and serves junk food and yet there are many who have been eating in this restaurant for years. Why?
There is no other restaurant nearby and over the years they've got immuned to the bad service and amazingly developed an irresistible taste for the junk food. In life, if you have no choice then you have no choice but to develop a liking for what you have.

*

First Timer: "The service in this restaurant is very bad."
Regular: "Wait till you eat the food."

*

The food was so bad I wanted to complain to the manager, but I didn't have the time to queue up, so I left.

*

Customer: "The food is terrible here, I'd like to see the manager."
Waiter: "Sorry sir, the manager is not in."
Customer: "How about your chef?"
Waiter: "In fact sir, both of them are out for lunch."

*

My favourite restaurant hires only married men. They are so used to taking orders that too with a beaming smile.

*

Disgusted diner: "What do you call this stuff, coffee or tea?"
Waiter: "What do you mean, sir?"
Diner: "It tastes like paraffin!"
Waiter: "Well, if tastes like paraffin, it must be coffee. Our tea tastes like turpentine."
(Believe me. That's how coffee and tea taste in most government hospitals)

*

Customer: "Do you serve crabs here?
Waiter: "We serve everyone, please have a seat."

*

Customer: "Do you serve nuts here?"
Waiter: "We serve nuts as well as crabs here, please have a seat."

*

Diner: "I'll have what the man in the next table is having."
Waiter: "Sorry sir, that would certainly infuriate him and we don't practise such things in this restaurant."

*

Diner: "There's a worm in my soup." The waiter, trying to cover up, said, "That's not a worm, sir. That's our specialty. It's a tiny winy sausage."

*

Diner: "There are dead flies in my soup." The quick thinking waiter replied, "Those are black raisins dressed to look like flies."

*

Waiter: "We have boiled tongues, fried kidneys and frog legs."
Puzzled diner: "Why do they employ such people here?"

*

Why are they called waiters and waitresses?
Because the keep their customers **waiting** indefinitely.

*

Diner: "Can I have your cook's photograph and particulars, please."
Waiter: "Are you going to publish his photograph in a magazine?"
Diner: "I would like his photograph and particulars to appear in the Guinness Book of World Records as the most tasteless cook in the world!"

*

Diner: "Waiter, this soup isn't fit for a pig!"
Waiter: "I'll take it back and get some that is."

*

Diner: "Waiter, this soup tastes funny."
Waiter: "How come you are not laughing?"
Diner: "Well, I'm just trying to control myself just like all the other diners!"

*

Customer: "I want to have a really good meal. What would you recommend?"
Waiter: "The restaurant just across the road."

*

Disgusted diner: "Do I have to wait till I die of starvation?"
Waiter: "No sir, we close at eight."

*

Miscellaneous – Part 2

When all the living ex-presidents and the current president of America are in a boat and the boat sinks. Who will be saved?
The United States of America.

*

How do you fight poverty?
By throwing stones at beggars.

*

What would the world be without men?
Free of crime and full of lesbians.

*

He strongly believes in women's liberty particularly for those involved in the world's oldest profession. He insists, "They must be free and should not charge a single cent."

*

A wise man once said, "Never stand between a dog and a lamp post."

*

What is it that a man can't do but a dog can?
A man can't but a dog can lick its own balls.

*

What did the cannibal say when he saw a train full of passengers?
Very delighted, he said, "That's a real chew-chew train."

*

A hooker laments, "Business has been so bad lately that I have to end up working for free to keep practising my trade and to retain my regular customers. Besides, age is catching up with me."
Acquaintance: "By the way, how old are you?"
Hooker: "I've been telling my customers I'm 25 years old for the past 40 years."

*

<u>A wage earner's frustration</u>
Every time he tries to make ends meet, the ends get elongated.

*

When a student fails to prepare for his examination, he is actually preparing to fail.

*

What is life?
Life is actually a bed of roses full of thorns.

*

Robber: "Your money or your life?
Man: "Look, I only have 50 cents in my wallet. Do you want to end up a murderer for a miserable 50 cents?"
Robber: "Get lost"

*

Contraceptives should be used on all conceivable occasions.

*

Silence or keeping your mouth shut builds up the pressure. That's why men fart more times a day than women.

*

Whether male or female, which is the profession that helps you fart the least a day?
The teaching profession.

*

We have heard of a hen-pecked husband. Ever heard of a cock-pecked wife? No, only cock-pricked ones.

*

Son: "Mum, can I have a puppy for Christmas?"
Mum: "Of course not. You'll have turkey just like the rest of us."

*

Describe an unkempt bachelor's flat. A flat where the plants are all dead. But there's something growing in the fridge.

*

He doesn't know the meaning of fear. He's too afraid to ask.

*

Many people have seen King Kong play table tennis but he swears he doesn't play table tennis and insists that the only game he plays is ping pong.

*

What's the difference between a musician and a dead rodent?
One composes and the other decomposes.

*

You are such a cold-blooded person, if the deadliest mosquito bit you it would die of pneumonia!

*

A foreigner visiting a remote village was very eager to swim in the river. He asked the boys playing near the river, "Are there sharks in this river?"
The boys said, "No sharks."
He jumped into the river and was happily swimming. To be doubly sure he called and asked the boys, "Are you sure there are no sharks in this river?"
The boys replied, "No sharks, only crocodiles."

*

Ever heard of a florist who had two children?
One a budding genius and the other a blooming idiot.

*

How many of them work in this office?
About a quarter of them. Another quarter laze around and the remaining half sleep on the job.

*

"Do you know deep breathing kills germs?"
"Oh really? How do you get them to breathe deeply?"

*

"Does this band take request?"
"Certainly."
"Good. I request they stop playing!"

*

Jason: "I bet I know where you are going tonight."
Simon: "If you could guess correctly, I'll pay you $10 or you pay me $20."
Jason: "To sleep!"

*

Woman at the door: "You were supposed to come yesterday to repair the doorbell."
Repairman: "I did. I rang the bell five times but got no answer, so I left."

*

How can you make a witch scratch?
Take away her 'W'.

How can you make a bitch scratch?
Rip her off her '**B**'.

*

Do you use your right hand or your left hand to write?
I use either a pen or a pencil.

*

Two little boys were looking at an abstract painting in an art shop.
"Let's run," said one, "before they say we did it."

*

Smart ghosts walk through walls. The stupid ones climb over.

*

She's a very shy person. She covers the bird cage when she undresses and covers the mirror when she takes her bath.

*

Friend 1: "You dance beautifully."
Friend 2: "I wish I could say the same for you."
Friend 1: "You could if you were as big a liar as I am!"

*

A man in the sea: "Help, help, I can't swim."
A drunk on the shore shouted back, "I too can't swim, am I complaining?"

*

Two thieves returned home after robbing a big bank.
Said the first thief, "Let's see how much we've got."
Second thief: "I'm tired. Let's find out how much we
robbed from the morning papers."

*

Rattling good time - Two skeletons happily dancing for a
fast beat on top of a tin roof.

*

"Are you sure your neighbour's daughter who has been
making a pass at you is so thin?"
"You won't believe it. She can play hide-and-seek behind
a flag pole!"

*

John: "I want to fight air pollution. But how am I to go
about doing it?"
Peter: "You could start by not breathing!"

*

Who is that guy behaving so strangely?
A total stranger.

*

Only vampires know that blood is thicker, tastier and more
intoxicating than red wine.

*

Beware of dogs. Don't trust cats either.

*

While driving, a bus driver died peacefully in his sleep unlike his passengers who were screaming and yelling.

*

A young boy was looking admiringly and smiling at a very sexy and beautiful girl who was a few years older than he was. Amused, the girl told him, "I know what you are thinking." The boy eagerly asked, "Will you allow me to do what I am thinking?"

*

Researchers have painstakingly discovered that everyone born in this world is unique just like every other person.

*

After the long winded extremely boring job orientation, the lone oriental person in the group got disoriented.

*

If people from Poland are called Poles, why aren't people from Holland called Holes?

*

It has recently been discovered that research causes cancer in rats.

*

A happy bull terrier is one with four legs and one arm in his mouth.

*

Dog for Sale
Eats anything and is fond of children and adult's neck and posterior.

*

A philosopher is a calm and collected person who is very philosophical about other people's life and only gets worked up with his own.

*

Research Scholar: "Why do overlook and oversee mean opposite things?"
English Professor: "When you oversee something you tend to overlook certain things which would be considered an oversight and this means even oversight and oversee mean opposite things. But look, see and sight mean the same thing. Have I confused you enough for your thesis?"
Research Scholar: "I've decided to give up doing my research!"

*

Multi-tasking means screwing up several things at one go, single handedly.

*

Jason is always late for work, but he makes it up by leaving early.

*

Income Tax Department

We've got what it takes to take what you've got much to your ire and consternation.

*

Where are hell drivers heading?
To hell!

*

A little girl seeing a snake for the first time, called her mother, "Mummy, come quickly, there's a tail moving without a body in the garden."

*

A man sitting in a train chewing gum, smiled politely to the old lady seated opposite him. Said the lady, "Young man, thank you for trying to politely strike a conversation with me but I am deaf."

*

None of the players smoked, yet the football coach gave every player a lighter because they kept losing all their matches.

*

Researchers were amazed to discover that a bee flying towards its beehive was the first to use the following words before human beings did: "Honey, I'm home."

*

What has a bottom at the top?
A leg.

*

What keeps getting a bottom on it?
A chair (not to forget toilet bowls).

*

What did one eye say to the other eye?
Something's come between us that smells.

*

My husband is a liver, brain and joint specialist."
"Oh, is he a doctor?"
"No, a butcher."

*

John: "My wife can cook, but doesn't."
Jason: "Don't feel bad. My wife can't cook, but
does."

*

What do you think of elephant trunks?
Are they going to look any better with suit cases or hand
bags?

*

What do you call a sleeping bull?
A bulldozer.

*

They say children brighten a home.
May be because they always forget to turn off the TV and lights.

*

Wilfred: "Bernard's eyes are so big I suppose they are bigger than his brains."
Ivan: "Don't be silly. How could his eyes be bigger than something he doesn't have?"

*

Barber: "Haven't I shaved you before, sir?"
Customer: "No, I got this scar during a violent scuffle with my ex-wife."

*

Money is called cold cash because it doesn't stay in your pocket long enough to get warm.

*

Researchers have discovered that those who exercise vigorously, die earlier but healthier.

*

Steven: "Clarence, you keep telling people that you are twenty-one years old and I've noticed you've been saying that for the past eight years."
Clarence: "I'm not the sort of person who says one thing today and another thing tomorrow!"

*

Judge: "Why did you steal the car?"
Accused: "It was parked in front of a cemetery
and I thought that the owner was dead."
Judge: "But by now you should have realized that the
owner is alive."
Accused: "Yes and I'm shocked."
Judge: "But please compose yourself and don't be
shocked to know that you are imprisoned for two years!"

*

Neighbour: "Your son threw a stone at me from behind."
Father: "Did the stone hit you?"
Neighbour: "Luckily, it didn't."
Father: "Then the person who threw the stone at you is
not my son. My son never misses."

*

My elder sister can sing, but she doesn't. My younger
sister can't sing, but she does.

*

Patient: "I keep thinking I'm a dog."
Doctor: "Well, I have no choice but to refer you to a vet."

*

Judge: "Have you been arrested before?"
Accused: "No. This is the first time I've been caught."

*

Little boy: "Sally, my daddy and mummy are not at home.
Are your parents at home?
Little Sally: "My parents are not at home."
Little boy: "Wow, that's great. Why don't you
come over to my house and we can play."
Little Sally: "Play what?"
Little boy: "Let's play daddy and mummy."

*

Doctor: "You only have six hours to live. Is there anyone
you would like to see?"
Patient: "Yes, another doctor."

*

Crime doesn't pay unless, of course, you do it well, don't
get caught and have amassed a huge wealth.

*

"What are you doing in my tree, young man?"
"One of your apples fell down and I'm putting it back".

*

They say barking dogs seldom bite. When a dog is barking
how the heck could it bite. Just like a human being a dog
can't perform two acts at one time.

*

Dogs are Man's best friends because the human friends a
man has can back stab them but dogs don't. The farthest
a dog can go is to bite or scratch a man's back.

*

Why do dogs love wetting lamp posts? Over several generations, dogs have come to sense that lamp posts don't complain.

*

"Your puppy just bit me in the ankle."
"Well, you don't expect my poor little thing to bite you on the neck, do you?"

*

"So you flunked your history exam." "It was truly disgusting. All the questions were about things that happened before I was born and some were about places I have never been to."

*

"Why do you roll your own cigarettes?"
"My doctor told me I needed exercise."

*

A visitor to a graveyard apprehended the undertaker of the graveyard.
Visitor: "Your signboard indicates that only honest men are buried in this graveyard. Then how come you have weathermen, lawyers, fortune tellers, cashers, accountants and politicians also buried in this graveyard?"
Undertaker: "The relatives of these men lied to us that they were honest men and got them buried here."
Visitor: "From now on be extra careful and make sure none of those relatives are buried here."

*

A three year old walked over to a pregnant lady while waiting with his mother in the doctor's office. He inquisitively asked the lady, "Why is your stomach so big?" She replied, "I'm having a baby." With big eyes, he asked, "Is the baby in your stomach?" She said, "He sure is." Then the little boy, with a puzzled look, asked, "Is it a good baby?" She said, "Oh, yes. It's a real good baby." With an even more surprised and shocked look, he asked, "Then why did you eat him?"

*

Old ladies are very fussy. Don't help them cross the road just leave them in the middle.

*

Employer to employee, "James, I'm not ordering you to do what I just said. It is just a suggestion. You don't have to do it unless you want to keep your job."

*

The height of frustration for an employer is when the best man for a job calls after the position has been filled.

*

"You should have been here at eight o'clock."
"Why boss, what happened? Anything interesting?"

*

A tactful employee hoping he would get a promotion soon sends his female boss 25 roses on her 45th birthday.

*

Money doesn't grow on trees but then why do banks have so many branches?

*

What's the difference between an ordinary man and superman?
An ordinary man wears his underwear inside his not so tight fitting pants. Superman outshines an ordinary man by wearing his shinny underwear outside (over) his tight fitting pants. (Poor soul there's no room for him to wear his underwear inside his tight fitting pants).

*

Two deaf met in a coffee shop and one of the deaf was carrying a fishing rod.
Deaf A: "Are you going fishing?'
Deaf B: "No, I'm going fishing."
Deaf A: "Oh, I thought you were going fishing."
Deaf B: "Oh no, I'm going fishing."

*

"Did the movie have a happy ending?"
"Oh yes, everyone was so glad it was over and was so happily rushing out of the theatre."

*

"Stop acting like a fool!"
"I'm not acting."

*

"What would you do if you were in my shoes?"
"I'll throw your smelly shoes away."

*

A young female politician was making house calls during an election campaign. She knocked at a door and told the person who opened the door, "Please support me." The man said, "I'm married with three kids. Why don't you try your luck with the guy living next door. He's very rich. He should be able to take you in and provide you with food and accommodation. If you are lucky, he might even marry you."

*

He's an excellent mathematics teacher. He clearly understands what he teaches only the students don't.

*

Where can you find love, bliss, wealth, health and serenity? Where does death come before life, divorce come before marriage and Thursday come before Wednesday and where can you find happiness and money all the time?
In the dictionary.

*

If a woman remains silent for an hour; rest assured she is dump and if she is beautiful marry her and lead a happy married life.

*

In a particular third world country trains (bound for different destinations) don't arrive on time and their arrivals are almost all the time delayed by hours. An impatient passenger asked the station master, "It's almost 9.00 p.m.; what time will the 5.30 p.m. train arrive?" The station master replied, "For your information, there are passengers out there still waiting for the 2.30 p.m. train. Please be patient."

*

Skipping is a good form of exercise and helps you reduce weight. It helps you skip breakfast, skip lunch, skip dinner and skip supper.

*

An apple a day keeps the doctor away. An onion a day keeps everyone away from you.

*

Before: A friend in need is a friend in deed.
Now: A friend not in need is a friend in deed

*

A few friends were happily chatting away and enjoying their drinks in a bar. There was "an odd man out" in the group who after two hours started to brag. He said, "Unlike you guys, I don't smoke, drink, womanise or gamble." Irritated, one of the guys in the group retorted, "You don't seem to have any of those wonderful habits, why the heck do you have to live then. Take the elevator to the 40th floor of this building and jump down. If you can't bring yourself to do it, we'll help you. What are friends for anyway?"

*

Little Johnny and Susie, each five years old, were playing house. They both decided it was time they get married. So Little Johnny went to Susie's dad to ask for her hand in marriage. "Where will you live?" asked Susie's dad, thinking this was cute. "Well," said Little Johnny, "I figured I could just move into Susie's room. It's plenty big for both of us. "And how will you live?" "I get $5 a week allowance and Susie gets $5 a week allowance. That should be enough." Getting exasperated since Little Johnny seems to know all the answers. Susie's dad asked, "And what if little ones come along?" "Well," said Little Johnny, "we've been lucky so far!"

*

Puppy love leads to a dog's life. People scorn at you and dogs bark at you.

*

Who is that guy behaving and blabbering like a mad person?
A psychiatrist gone mad.

*

By chance he discovered a permanent cure for amnesia but kept forgetting what it was.

*

"How did you get that black eyes?"
"Her husband caught me hiding under the bed."

*

I'm very particular about table manners. I'll never stir my coffee with my hand. I use a spoon.

*

What does a man do standing up, a woman sitting down and a dog on three legs?
Your guess is as good as mine!

*

What does a man do standing up, a woman sitting down and a dog on three legs?
Oh no, not that! The man stood up to pull up his zip, the woman was sitting down gossiping and the dog was scratching the posterior of a woman who was squatting down mending a flower pot.

*

He is so old, he easily gets tired brushing his dentures.

*

An annoyed father said, "Sam, you promised to clean your room and make the bed and if you didn't, didn't I promise to cane you?" Sam, after a long pause, put it very gently to his father, "Dad, since I broke my promise, you don't have to keep yours."

*

Doctor: "This is a very delicate operation and very honestly your chances of survival would only be 10%."
Patient: "Is that supposed to mean that if I don't undergo the operation, I'm left with no choice but to die?"
Patient's friend, an undertaker, said eagerly, "But if you die you have the luxury of three choices. You can be buried, cremated or thrown into the sea."

*

Dentists wear masks in order to protect themselves from wide open stinking mouths of their patients.

*

There is something a dentist can't say to his patient - "Shut your stinking mouth!"

*

A ninety-three year old lady officially changed her name to Angel so that when she dies she could go to heaven.

*

Three blockheads, eager to taste wine for the first time in their lives, went to a wine shop and after spending almost an hour, left the shop without buying a single bottle of wine because there was no expiry date in any of the bottles.

*

You never know what you can do till you try and after trying you'll come to realize the truth that you are not good at whatever you had tried.

*

Raymond: "I just underwent an operation. The tumor in my brain was successfully removed."
Jeffrey: "How could they remove a tumor from something you don't have?"

*

Wife: "My favourite umbrella is missing. Did you take my umbrella to the office this morning?"
Husband: "No, I took the bus."

*

Once a year we are all reminded what we really are on 1st April. That's too gentle a reminder. We probably should be reminded every month so that some of us could take the effort to buck up.

*

James: "How old are you John?"
John: "I have been 25 years old for the past 28 years. I refused to grow up after the age of 25."
James: "It's amazing John, you really don't look 53. You look much older despite refusing to grow up."

*

Unknown to many, Santa Claus's real name is Mr. Christmas and his wife's name is Mrs. Mary Christmas.

*

Two fleas were so tired to walk, so they frantically waited at the side of a road to take a lift from a dog.

*

Jason fell over twenty feet but luckily did not get hurt. It was dark and he was actually trying to get to his seat in a cinema.

*

It's an irony that you have no choice but to scratch yourself because no one else knows where you itch.

*

It is not advisable to drink and drive because if you are speeding and have to suddenly apply the brake, you might spill your drink.

*

A Defence Minister is a strong believer in operational readiness and is always ready to lay done his army officers' and soldiers' lives for the country.

*

A Concorde plane which had just taken off boasted to the birds flying near by, "You can't fly as fast as I can." Irritated, one of the birds snapped, "We certainly can if we were inside you!"

*

Son: "Mum, how do monkeys behave?"
Mother: "Just like my mother-in-law. I mean like your grandma, Betty."

*

Suddenly there was a big crowd gathered in a remote village and the villagers were looking up at the sky astounded and yelling:
"Is that a dog flying?"
"Is that a pig flying?"
"Is that a donkey flying?"
"Is that a monkey flying?"
The lone visiting city dweller with a binoculars exclaimed, "No, it is superwoman!"

*

Why don't superman and superwoman get married?
They both harbour the same fear. If they got married and had to undress to make love, they fear that people might steal their outfits and fly away leaving them grounded for life.

*

A furious father entered the principal's room and blasted, "I'm flabbergasted. The teacher hit my son and you have expelled my son instead of expelling the teacher from school!"
Principal: "The teacher hit your son in self-defence."

*

Son: "Dad, can you help me find the lowest common denominator in this problem."
Dad: "When I was a student, I tried and gave up. I'm surprised they have not found it yet."

*

How do you make a sausage roll?
Just use your finger to flick it and the sausage will roll.

*

Interviewer: "You should be aware that the famous Captain Chef made five voyages and in which one of the voyages was he killed?"
Job applicant, applying for the position of Marine Engineer, replied, "In his fourth voyage."
Interviewer: "How come it's not his fifth voyage?"
Job applicant: "Well, his fifth voyage was his funeral voyage back home."

*

Wilfred: "My frog can jump higher than your house."
Jonathan: "Ha, Ha, Ha, stop kidding me."
Wilfred: "Yes, my frog certainly can."
Jonathan: "Okay, if your frog can jump higher than my house, I pay you $20. If it can't, you pay me $40."
Wilfred agreed to the bet and made his frog jump.
Jonathan: "Ha, Ha, Ha, your frog didn't even jump my knee level. I won the bet."
Wilfred: "If you can make your house jump slightly higher than my frog, you win the bet, if you can't, I win."

*

A guy went to the optician to make his first pair of spectacles. He returned home, sat on the sofa and asked the person seated opposite, "Honey, how do you find my new glasses?" The woman, controlling her laughter, told him that his house was across the road.

*

A guy anticipating a quiet, serene and romantic outing brought his girl friend to a cemetery. The surprised girl blurted out, "Of all the places you have brought me to a cemetery!" The guy replied, "This is truly a wonderful place and you don't seem to realize that people are dying to come here."

*

A mother was travelling in a plane with her four children. After the plane took off, her kids started running around and playing. The mother, engrossed reading a book, told her children to go out and play.

*

Frankie was feeling homesick (sick of home) and his mother sent him to his aunt's house.

*

What makes a road broad?
The letter 'B'.

*

What did the envelope say to the stamp?
"Stick with me baby, we'll go places."
And what was the stamp's reply?
"We won't go places instead we'll end up in one address, you stupid!"

*

Teacher: "Do fishes perspire?"
Student: "They certainly do, if not the sea won't be so salty."

*

Mother: "Alfred, are you going out to play with your torn trousers?"
Alfred: "No, with the kids across the street."

*

Melvin: "Oliver, have you come across guys who shave more than ten times a day?"
Oliver: "They must be crazy."
Melvin: "No, they are barbers."

*

Nervous breakdown is a disorder parents acquire from their teenage children.

*

A vegetarian is a person who refuses to eat meat in public.

*

A father returning from work asked his son, "What's on TV tonight?" The son replied, "As usual, the fish bowl and the lamp."

*

A lady asked an artist, "Do you paint people in the nude?"
Artist: "I always paint with my clothes on."

*

I didn't come here to be insulted.
Where do you usually go then?

*

Football Manager: "Jason, you really played a great game."
Jason: "Please sir, I know how badly I played."
Manager: "No, you really played an excellent game for the other side."

*

Tom: "Dad, can you do my arithmetic for me?"
Dad: "No son, that won't be right."
Tom: "Never mind if it's wrong, so long as it's done."

*

Benjamin: "Mum, did you notice your hair is greying."
Mother: "You are so naughty and that's why my hair is greying."
Benjamin: "Oh dear, I can't imagine how mischievous and unruly you had been Mum. Grandma's hair is completely white!"

*

Beggar: "I haven't had more than one meal a day the whole of this week."
Fat lady: "That's amazing. How I wish I had your will power."

*

Alice: "Don't you think I sing with feeling?"
Alfred: "If you had feeling, you wouldn't sing."

*

Teacher: "Roland, I told you to draw a ring and you have drawn a square."
Roland: "I actually drew a boxing ring."

*

You can underestimate a fool but never underestimate the combine stupidity and power of a large group of fools. Run for your live.

*

Three snobbish rich men met in a posh hotel.
The 1st one said, "I'm planning to buy all the goldmines in the world."
The 2nd one replied, "I have no plans of selling them."
The 3rd one snapped, "If I stopped buying all the gold from these mines, what's the point buying or owning them."

*

What do most mothers do for a headache?
They send their children out to play.

*

Who gets a sack every time he goes to work?
The postman.

*

What gets wetter the more it dries?
A towel.

*

A blockhead engaged the services of a call girl. After he was done, he asked her, "Am I the first man you have ever slept with?" She said, "Yes," and the blockhead's happiness knew no bounds.

*

A guy fell head over heals for a blonde and lost his balance. His bank balance.

*

He wanted to become a comedian but decided not to because he was afraid that people might start laughing at him.

*

Did Adam and Eve have a date?
No, they had an apple.

*

Which part of a cake is the left side?
The part that is not eaten yet.

*

Why did John take a bicycle to bed?
Because he didn't want to walk in his sleep.

*

How did Adrian lose his hair?
He lost his hair by constantly worrying about losing his hair.

*

Where do life-threatening doctors and undertakers like to swim?
In the Dead Sea.

*

Teacher: "What makes the Tower of Pisa, lean?"
Student: "May be due to constant dieting."

*

What is yours which is used more by others than you yourself?
Your name.

*

Teacher: "How many sides a circle has?"
Student: "Two. The inside and the outside."

*

A guy was beginning to get bored with his blind date. He excused himself and went the wash room. When he returned to the table, he told her, "I have some bad news. My grandfather just passed away. I have to rush home." "Thanks heavens," said the girl, "If yours hadn't, mine would have had to."

*

Where did Batman find Robin?
In a pet shop.

*

A not very intelligent receptionist received a call. The caller asked, "Can I speak to Richard please?" The receptionist said, "Mr. Richard is on a two-week vacation, would you like to hold?"

*

Mother: "Benny, how come you have not tidied your room?"
Benny: "I'm tired."
Mother: "You're lazy. Hard work never killed anyone."
Benny: "I don't want to run the risk of being the first."

*

What do you call a snake that works for the government? A civil serpent.

*

Fred: "Is your mother one of those women who lie about her age?"
Jack: "Not really. She would say she is as old as dad and lie about his age."

*

Alice: "My aunty was so embarrassed when she was asked to take off her mask at a party."
Susie: "But why?"
Alice: "She wasn't wearing one."

*

Fat man: "You look as though you've lived through a famine."
Thin man: "And you look as if you've caused one."

*

What can be broken without dropping, hitting or smashing?
A promise.

*

Clifford: "I know an author who took ten years to finish a book."
Donald: "That's nothing. I know a prisoner who took twenty years to finish a sentence."

*

What is a secret?
A secret is something you tell one person at a time and request the person to keep it a secret.

*

If a secret becomes the talk of the town, what is it called?
An open secret.

*

Judge: "Have you ever been cross-examined before?"
Accused: "Yes, Your Honour. Several times. I'm a married man."

*

Which word is pronounced, spelt and written wrongly even by well-educated people?
The word, "wrongly".

*

The younger sister noticed her elder sister applying cream on her face. The younger one asked the elder one, "Why are you applying cream on your face?" The elder one replied, "To make my face look more beautiful." Later, the elder sister removed the cream and washed her face. The younger one looked pathetically at her sister and said glumly, "It doesn't really work, does it?"

*

Which nails cannot be used to hit with a hammer?
Fingernails.

*

Why do leopards never attempt to escape from the zoos?
They know they could easily be spotted.

*

What can fall on water without getting wet?
A shadow.

*

Where can you find money when you need it urgently?
In the dictionary.

*

What's good on bread and bad on the road?
Jam.

*

Which jam cannot be spread on breads?
Traffic jam.

*

Why do you look confused?
A joke a friend told me yesterday about a banana peel keeps slipping my mind..

*

Mary: "I'm very shy to tell you that I've been asked to marry several times."
Shirley: "By whom?"
Mary: "My mum and dad."

*

He was so ugly the call girl had to politely decline by saying that she had a headache.

*

The worst thing that can spoil a woman's mood in a party is when she notices another woman wearing the same dress she is wearing. If a man happened to be in a similar situation, he would be pleasantly surprised and would approach the other guy to find out where he bought his clothes. Is this one of the many reasons why a man is called a gentleman?

*

The weaker sex is the stronger sex because of the weakness of the stronger sex for the weaker sex.

*

Women are not heartless all the time. They can be very forgiving at times especially when they are in the wrong.

*

The best oral contraceptive for a young girl is the word 'No'.

*

Woman was God's second mistake and almost every married woman regrets having married the worst man in the world, God's first mistake.

*

The only time a wife doesn't interrupt her husband is when he talks in his sleep.

*

Who are those women who will not ask a man to shut his mouth?
Female dentists.

*

What is retirement?
Stepping aside to let a young, less experienced but bright, energetic, better educated and more capable person to take over your position.

*

A guy reputed for giving a very boring motivational talk for three hours found no one interested in attending his talk. He then thought of a plan and struck a deal with several doctors. These doctors sent all their patients suffering from insomnia for the three hour talk for a reasonably high fees. All the patients who attended his talk were cured of insomnia and the speaker and doctors laughed all the way to the bank.

*

Judge: "You are sentenced to spend three days in jail."
Accused: "What's the charge?"
Judge: "There isn't any charge. You get to stay in jail for free."

*

A police officer complimenting a housewife said, "Madam, it was very brave of you to attack a burglar at night when it was so dark." Though embarrassed, she smiled and accepted the compliment but had to keep the reason for her bravery a secret. She, in fact, didn't know it was a burglar. She thought it was her husband returning home late.

*

A department store which sells bras has African, Chinese and Russian sizes. The African sizes uplift the fallen, the Chinese sizes make mountains out of molehills and the Russian sizes suppress the masses.

*

Miser: "How much for a hair cut?"
Barber: "Eight dollars."
Miser: "How much for a shave?"
Barber: "New blade two dollars, used blade one dollar."
Miser: "Okay, shave my head and face with a used blade."

*

What kind of medical condition do most nudist suffer from?
Clothesrophobia.

*

Which is the bow that cannot be tied with a string?
Rainbow.

*

Wilfred was so busy he had no time to mow his lawn. So he bought two **"lawn moovers"** and the two cows turned out to be a double joy for him. He now gets fresh milk free of charge.

*

When does a woman care for a man's company?
When he owns one.

*

A drunkard was staggering in the park when he came across a man doing push up. Shakily he bent down and said, "Excuse me sir, have you been keeping your eyes closed. Your girl is no more under you."

*

Fussy old lady: "How far is the hospital from here?"
Passer-by: "About 10 km away."
Fussy old lady: "Oh my god, I need to get to the hospital fast."
Another passer-by: "I tell what. Just close your eyes and cross the road, you'll get there in no time."

*

What is it that breaks when you throw it on a politician's face?
Egg.

*

What is it that doesn't break when you throw it on a particular American President's face?
Shoe.

*

Why don't cannibals eat clowns?
Because they taste funny.

*

He lent his friend $10,000 for a plastic surgery and now can't recognize him.

*

A lady said she was 29 years old but she looked like a person born 10 years before World War I.

*

Wife to husband, "Darling, take off your glasses and you'll look very handsome." Husband takes off his glasses and tells his wife, "Darling, you too look very beautiful now."

*

Timothy: "Roland, you don't seem to have any luck with all your blind dates. What's wrong with you?"
Roland: "Nothing is wrong with me. Surprisingly every one of these girls happens to suffer from speech impediment."
Timothy: "What's that?"
Roland: "None of them could say 'yes'."

*

What is six inches long and two inches wide and drives women crazy?
Money.

*

What do blondes and the Bermuda Triangle have in common?
One swallows semen, the other seamen.

*

A five year old boy: "Dad, I want to marry."
Father: "Marry whom?"
Boy: "Grandma."
Father: "You can't marry my mother."
Boy: "When you can marry my mother, why can't I marry yours?"

*

John is meticulous, forward thinking and always plans well ahead for the future. Instead of one, he buys six cases of beer.

*

What are the three things people never eat before breakfast?
Lunch, dinner and supper.

*

Why do office staff avoid drinking coffee at work?
Because it keeps them awake.

*

Rodney: "Yesterday I had a row with my girl friend."
Roger: "Why, what happened?.
Rodney: "I wanted to bring her to the stadium to watch a football match. But she wanted to watch a movie."
Roger: "So, how was the movie?"

*

Why did the stupid man put ice in his condom?
To keep the swelling down.

*

Why did Robson pee in the ladies toilet?
Because he wanted to go where no man had ever gone to pee.

*

Why does a chicken lay eggs?
Because instead of laying, if it dropped it, it would break.

*

James: "Nancy, have you noticed that whenever John coughs or sneezes he covers his mouth with a handkerchief. That's good manners."
Nancy: "He actually covers his mouth to make sure his dentures don't fall off."

*

The basement wall was cracking and Stanley's father couldn't afford to fix it. Disappointed, Stanley went around telling his school mates that he came from a broken home.

*

Teacher: "What do you mean by filthy rich?
Student: "A person who is very rich with no bathtubs in his house."

*

Mother: "Why are you taking a ruler to bed with you?"
Son: "To see how long I sleep."

*

Simon: "How I wished I were in your shoes."
Raymond: "Why would you want to be in my shoes?"
Simon: "Mine are worn out and yours look brand new."

*

An insane bloke is so glad his parents named him James because that's what everyone calls him much to his astonishment and pleasant surprise.

*

The same insane bloke was surprised to know that his father and mother were married on the same day. He says, "What a coincidence."

*

Jason: "Susan, you are such a sweet person, I bought these sweets for you."
Susan: "How sweet of you. I also bought something for you."
Jason: "Oh, really."
Susan: "These nuts are for you."

*

In a pub, beauty is in the eyes of the beer holder.

*

Simon: "If you don't marry me, I'll blow my brains out!"
Betty: "Don't be ridiculous. How could you blow out something you don't have?"

*

Brian: "Fish is brain food and I eat it all the time to develop my brains."
Desmond: "Why do eat something all the time to develop something you don't have!"

*

1st Neighbour: "Last night I had the best dream in my entire life which made me very happy."
2nd Neighbour: "What was it?"
1st Neighbour: "I dreamt your entire family was moving out to a far-off place."

*

Alice: "I want to commit suicide."
Cindy: "But why?"
Alice: "Mathew said I am as ugly as you are."

*

Sister: "What are you going to give me for my birthday?"
Brother: "Close your eyes and tell me what you see."
Sister: "I see nothing."
Brother: "Well, that's what you are going to get for your birthday from me."

*

Customer: "I would like some rat poison."
Overworked pharmacist absent mindedly asked: "Would you like to have it here?"

*

An Indian proverb says, "You bathe your dog, clean it up and feed dog chow. When you unleash it, it runs out looking for shit to eat."

*

John: "Where were you born?"
Jack: "In a hospital."
John: "It's terrible to be sick on your very first day."

*

Who is prone to make a grave mistake?
An undertaker burying a body in the wrong place.

*

Desmond: "There was a ferocious lion roaring in front of me, a tiger on my left slowing approaching me and a leopard on my right, I almost fainted."
Jeremy: "How did you escape?"
Desmond: "I walked away from their cages."

*

Arnold: "During my hunting trip I spotted a leopard."
Jackson: "Stop kidding me. You can't spot a leopard. They are born with spots."

*

Sign in a sliming centre - **THE WORLD IS IN BAD SHAPE - MUST YOU BE TOO?**

*

Benson: "Whistling while you work, however happy you are, is a bad habit.
Norman: "My father whistles at work and he also whistles after work."
Benson: "That's strange."
Norman: "My father is a traffic police and a part time football referee."

*

A young lady went to a fortune teller to have her fortune told. "I will answer two questions for you for ten dollars," said the fortune teller. The young lady paid the fortune teller ten dollars then asked, "Don't you think ten dollars is a lot of money for two questions?" "I don't think so," answered the fortune teller, "Now, what is your second question?"

*

Why do cows have bells?
Because their horns don't work.

*

Harry: "I wish I had enough money to buy ten aeroplanes."
Larry: "Why in the whole white world will you need ten aeroplanes?"
Harry: "I don't need the planes, just the money."

*

A little boy went to the ballot for the first time with his father and watched the girls dance around on their toes for a while. Then he asked, "Why don't they just get taller girls?"

*

To err is human and to cover it up is being a better and cleverer human.

*

What did the bald man say when received a comb for his birthday?
He said, "Thank you very much. I'll never part with it."

*

Son: "Can worms be eaten?"
Father: "Certainly not. Why do you ask?"
Son: "There was one in the pie you just ate."

*

Sally: "Mum, what was the name of the last station the train stopped?"
Mother: "Don't disturb me, I'm reading."
Sally: "But I have to. Little Jimmy got off at that station."
Mother: "What?"

*

Nancy: "How was your date?"
Susan: "This guy has a small, flat nose."
Nancy: "Oh dear, how does he smell?"
Susan: "Terrible."

*

When I was young I didn't like going to weddings. My grandmother would tell me, "You're next." However, she stopped doing that after I started saying the same thing to her at funerals.

*

"Why were you driving so fast?" asked the policeman to the speeding motorist. The motorist replied, "Well, my brakes are faulty and I wanted to get home before I had an accident."

*

Fat lady: "I'd like to see a dress that could fit me."
Sales assistant: "So would I but we have none that could fit you. But don't lose hope. You can try your luck at the curtain shop just across the road."

*

A woman who plays hockey can easily beat a woman who plays football.

*

Mr. Mouse discovered Mrs. Mouse drowning in a bowl of water. He dragged her out and gave her mouse to mouse resuscitation.

*

A very religious father was explaining to his son how the fairies turned the leaves brown. The son gave his father a pathetic look and asked, "Haven't you ever heard of photosynthesis?"

*

120

Bald headed father: "When I was your age I had lovely wavy hair."
Son: "But when did the so called "wavy hair" bid farewell to you?"

*

An Irish woman expecting her sixth child was horrified to read in the newspaper that every sixth person born in the world is Chinese. However, in order to prevent any misunderstanding, she decided to keep the newspaper article to show her husband and others when the child is born.

*

Roy: "Why do you call me an idiot in front of others?"
Bob: "Sorry, I didn't know you wanted to keep it a secret."

*

Guest: "Your parrot appears to be very stiff and doesn't utter a word. Is it sick?"
Owner: "No, it's stuffed."

*

Alison: "Do you say your prayers before your dinner?"
Fiona: "I don't. My mother is a good cook."

*

Who is the most stupid pickpocket?"
The one who tries his luck in a nudist camp.

*

Which dog is the noblest of all?
The hot-dog. It feeds the hand that bites it.

*

What did the ice-cream say to the cake?
I'm superior to you. You are being eaten but I'm only being licked.

*

Why did the tomato blush?
Because it saw the salad dressing.

*

Men end up telling lies because women are persistent in asking too many questions.

*

Experience is what you get when you didn't get what you wanted.

*

Friends come and go, enemies accumulate.

*

To catch the bank robbers, the special squad police force guarded all the exits. The professional robbers escaped through the entrance.

*

What's a girl like you doing in a nice place like this?

*

Adam: "Evelyn, you remind me of a very popular film star."
Evelyn: "Oh really, which one?"
Adam: "Rin Tin Tin"

*

Teacher: "What do you like most?"
Lim Ah Chong: "I like flutes velly much."
Teacher: "Do you play the flute well?"
Lim Ah Chong: "No, I mean flutes like apples, bananas, pears and olanges."

*

Beatrice: "The good looking guy sitting over there is annoying me."
Janice: "Why? He's not even looking at you."
Beatrice: "I know and that's what is annoying me."

*

Sylvester: "When they take out your appendix, it's an appendectomy; when they take your tonsils out, it's a tonsillectomy. What is it, when they remove a growth from your head called?"
Wilkinson: "I don't know."
Sylvester: "It's called a hair-cut, stupid!"

*

Barry: "This band is disgusting and they play horrible music. They ought to be......."
Garry: "They ought to be what?"
Barry: "Banned."

*

An uneducated bloke was reading the newspaper upside down in a park. A passer-by pointed that out to him. The irritated bloke snapped: "This is something normal people can't do; only highly intelligent people like me can!"

*

There are so many dried leaves in the Garden of Eden. Those are Adam's discarded old clothes.

*

A lady passenger first time travelling in a ship was curious to know something. So she asked the ship captain, "Captain, do ships this size sink often?" The captain replied, "No madam, only once." She then asked, "You mean like the Titanic?" Replied the captain, "Well, you never know. It can be even worse than the Titanic."

*

Dorothy: "Is your husband dead?"
Margaret: "He died during a hunting trip years ago."
Dorothy: "How did he die?"
Margaret: "Well, he probably missed his shots and I suspect something he was running away from ate him."

*

What can run across the floor but has no legs?
Water.

*

Valerie: "What's the trouble with you, Michelle? You are always wishing for something you don't have."
Michelle: "What else can you wish for?"

*

What is it that holds water yet is full of holes?
A sponge.

*

Why will 2012 be a good year for kangaroos?
Because it will be a leap year.

*

Doctor: "How do you feel today?"
Patient: "Same as usual, with my hands."

*

What's another name for a smart duck?
A wise quacker.

*

What did the mother bee say to the baby bee?
"Don't be naughty honey, just beehive yourself while I comb your hair."

Why do white sheep eat more than black ones?
Because there are more white sheep in the world than black ones.

*

Mrs. Jones: "Have you told your little boy not to go around imitating me?"
Mrs. Simon: "Yes, I told him very firmly not to act like an idiot."

*

Teacher: "What is wind?"
Student: "Air in a hurry."

*

How do you make a cigarette lighter?
Take out the tobacco.

*

What is everybody in the world doing at the same time?
Growing older.

*

Which box can never keep a secret?
A chatterbox.

*

Why is a sleeping baby like a hijack?
Because it's a "kid-napping".

*

What is it that you can't see but is always before you?
The future.

*

What is it that you have difficulty seeing and is always behind you?
Your posterior.

*

What did the smoker who was sick and tired of reading that smoking was bad for health do?
He gave up reading.

*

Mother: "Why are you spanking Wilfred, dear?"
Father: "Because he's getting his school report tomorrow and I won't be here."

*

Geraldine: "Have you lived here all your life?"
Mabel: "Till this moment yes but I don't know if I'm going to live here all my life."

*

Who are the best book-keepers?
Those who never return the books they borrow.

*

Guest: "You have a large collection of books but you need more shelves."
House owner: "The problem is, it's so difficult to borrow shelves."

*

Benedict: "I'm sorry to hear that your factory was burnt down. What did your company manufacture?"
Dickson: "Fire extinguishers."

*

Humphrey: "Do you know I always get up when the first ray of sunlight shines at my window?
Jeffrey: "Isn't that rather early?"
Humphrey: "No, my room faces the west."

*

There were three men in a boat with four cigarettes but no lighter. What did they do to get a cigarette lighter? They threw out one cigarette and made the boat a cigarette lighter.

*

What ship has no captain but a male and a female?
Courtship.

*

Women's breasts are intended for children but men end up playing with them.

*

A girl on reaching home after spending the evening with her date, said, "Since we've been going Dutch all evening, you kiss yourself and I'll kiss myself."

*

Hillary phones Bill and says, "Honey, I'm pregnant."
There's a brief silence, then Bill asks, "Who's calling?"

*

How does Bill Clinton practise save sex?
By placing a guard outside his office door.

*

What do you get if you cross a former president with the present foreign secretary?
Chelsea Clinton.

*

A blockhead's girl friend broke off with him and wanted her photograph back. Frustrated, the blockhead collected several photographs of women from his friends and mailed the photographs to her with a note - "I don't know which one is you, please keep your photograph and return the others to me."

*

A newspaper reporter was interviewing a man on his ninety-ninth birthday. At the end of the interview he said cheerfully, "I hope I can come back to see you on your hundredth birthday." The old man replied, "Barring any unforeseen tragedy, I see no reason why you can't. You are young and look healthy to me."

*

A doctor calls from the hospital and asks,
"Are you the husband of Mrs. Dorothy?"
Husband: "Yes, I am."
Doctor: "I have good news and bad news for you."
Husband: "What's the bad news?"
Doctor: "Your wife met with an accident."
Husband: "What's the good news?"
Doctor: "She has become an angel."
Husband: "Oh my god. Where am I going to look for an undertaker?"
Doctor: "Leave that to me. I'll recommend you a friend."

*

What is artificial insemination?
The husband spares the rod and yet the wife gets pregnant.

*

Hard work will certainly pay off in the future. Laziness pays off immediately.

*

Rodney went to his friend's house and his friend's beautiful wife was serving him a delicious meal. Said Rodney, "You are not only stunningly beautiful, you are also a good cook." Said his friend's wife, "Rodney, I have to warn you that my husband will be back in two hours." Surprised, Rodney said, "But I'm not doing anything." Said his friend's wife, "All I'm telling you is you still have two hours."

*

Garry: "Haven't I seen you some place before?"
Alice: "Yes and that's why I don't go there anymore."

*

A young man noticed an old lady, he knew, sipping her coffee. He went, sat at her table, ordered a coffee and started chatting away with her. He noticed a bowl of peanuts and raisins and asked her if he could have some. She said, "Why not," and pushed the bowl to him. After a while, when he was about to leave he realized he had emptied the bowl and appologised profusely to the lady for not keeping some for her. "That's all right," replied the old lady and said, "Ever since I lost my teeth, all I can do is suck off the chocolate."

*

A guy went to a bar and ordered 10 pegs of whiskey on the rock. When served, he finished the 10 glasses in less than 15 minutes and ordered another 10 pegs. He again gulped the 10 pegs in less than 15 minutes. The shocked bartender approached him and said, "You drank so much whiskey in such a short time." The guy replied, "You'll do the same, if you had what I have." The bartender asked, "What do you have?" The guy answered, "Only two dollars."

*

Mother: "Were you the one who saved my little boy from drowning?"
Lifeguard: "Yes."
Mother: "Now, where are his socks, shoes and cap?"

*

A prisoner, about to be executed was asked what he would like to have for his last meal.
Prisoner: "Strawberries."
Jailer: "But they are out of season."
Prisoner: "I'll wait."
Jailer: "Well, it's not fair for us to keep you waiting so we'll get you either canned strawberries or strawberry juice.

*

A burglar broke into a house in the middle of the night. To his shock, the light was turned on and the owner stood before him with a golf stick. Before the burglar could utter a word, the owner said, "Look I have misplaced a hundred dollar note somewhere in the house. Let's search for it and if we found it, let's split fifty-fifty."

*

A little boy almost on the verge of tears, told the old man sitting beside him in a park, "I can't do those things which big boys do." The old man with a depressed look and tears rolling down, said, "Me too." "Me too," cried the guy seated nearby, "I'm an impotent." (The crux of the matter - too young to, too old to and unable to)

*

What a woman has and a man doesn't have?
Well, this question has nothing to do with the anatomy. Just the letters 'WO'.

*

What does a woman have in front that a cow has behind?
The letter 'W'.

*

Today is tomorrow's yesterday.
Tomorrow is the day after tomorrow's yesterday.
Yesterday is the day before yesterday's tomorrow.
Today is also yesterday's tomorrow.

*

Who is a pessimist?
He is one, when opportunity either knocks at the door or presses the door bell, complains about the noise.

*

A lecturer told his students how a good lecture should be. He said, "A good lecture is like a woman's dress. Long enough to cover all the important parts and short enough to arouse interest."

*

Bertram to a very rich friend, "If you can lend me $200,000 for me to start my new business, I'll be indebted to you for life."

*

A self-confident woman is one who believes that there is no such thing as a small matter which can't be blown out of proportion.

*

Is driving away customers a difficult job to do? No, says a taxi driver.

*

Car mechanic: "I couldn't repair your brakes. So I made your horn louder."

*

If an interviewer makes a paper aeroplane out of your application form it means you are not even short-listed for the job.

*

How to be a successful sales man?
If you can't convince your customers, confuse them and not to forget, target the naïve ones.

*

A guy realized it took a lot of will power to give up. So he gave up trying to give up smoking.

*

A hospital is a place where they wake you up at four in the morning to give you a sleeping tablet.

*

Big cats are not dangerous. But a little pussy can ruin a man's life.

*

The only thing Raymond ever took up in school was space.

*

If you lend your friend $20 and never see him again, its $20 well spent.

*

The Conservative Party propagates innovation, progress and new ideas but is still pondering over it.

*

Many people worry about what others think of them not realizing that others seldom think of them.

*

An infuriated girl tells her boyfriend, "The only difference between you and a bucket of shit is the bucket!"

*

He thinks a lieutenant commander is the lieutenant's wife.

*

He thought a teetotaler was the score-keeper at golf.

*

A blockhead thought "ping pong balls" was a disease of the testicles originated from China.

*

A stand-up comedian told his audience, "This will be my last joke." They were all so relieved.

*

Gerard said something and his boss couldn't stop laughing. Did he crack a joke? No, he asked for a raise.

*

High society people are those who spend money they haven't got to buy things they don't need to impress people they don't like.

*

Try not to keep up with the living standards of others. It's cheaper and wiser to drag them down to your level.

*

His mouth stinks and his body odour is unbearable. Who is he?
A filthy rich guy.

*

A person who says he drinks to forget, never forgets to drink.

*

There are two reasons why men stay all night in a pub and drink. They either have no wives to go home to or they have.

*

A drunk wanted to go to a topless bar and stumbled into a bar with no roof.

*

I miss my wife's cooking, as often as I can.

*

A wise man once said, "He who thinks he knows all doesn't know he doesn't and believes he does."

*

Two gays, before marriage, think love is a pain in the heart but after marriage they realize it's a constant pain in the posterior.

*

What is orgasm?
A village woman: "I've been married for 30 years but I don't know what it is. May be you should ask my husband because he always comes and I don't."

*

A ransom note read: "We have kidnapped your mother-in-law. If you don't pay the ransom we will send her back." The son-in-law rushed to pay the ransom and returned home a happy man.

*

Just as a wife is a pain in the neck; a mother-in-law is an endless pain in the posterior.

*

The happiest moment in a son-in-law's life is when his mother-in-law moves out permanently or becomes an angel.

*

Husband to wife: "Darling, you know something. I like your mother-in-law more than mine."

*

When you help a friend in trouble, he feels very obligated and faithfully remembers you when he's in trouble again.

*

Sometimes you feel enemies are better than friends because they don't keep bothering you for money.

*

Samson was such a naughty boy, his parents told the kids in the neighbourhood not to play with him.

*

What's a lazy guy's ambition?
To marry a rich girl who is too proud to let her husband work.

*

Why is little Johnny unhappy?
When he plays hide-and-seek with the other kids, nobody comes to find him.

*

A father very angry with his teenage son who was not good in his studies and kept failing his exams, told him, "I'll be retiring soon. I can't afford to pay for your studies till you become an old man. I'll need the retirement money for my old age."

*

If you are trying to kill time make sure it's your own and not someone else's.

*

If you open your mouth you make a fool of yourself. If you keep it shut you can fool a lot of people.

*

History keeps repeating itself because nobody bothers to read history, particularly politicians like Saddam Hussein and George Bush.

*

One night when he returned home he found his wife in bed with "his best friend". He shot his wife and sterilized his dog as a punishment.

*

A brand new dog chow was named "Woof" because it would be the only brand dogs could ask for by name. For the same reason the new brand of cat food was named "Meow".

*

A guy in a cemetery standing before a tombstone was crying uncontrollably saying, "Why do you have to die and make my life so miserable." A passer-by noticed him and asked, "Is he one of your brothers or a close relative?" The guy replied, "No, he's my wife's ex-husband." The passer-by then noticed another man standing in front of another tombstone and crying, "Why did you die and make my life so miserable." The passer-by asked the man, "Who is he?" The guy answered, "He's a friend who borrowed $500,000 from me and I'm completely broke now and couldn't recover a single cent form him."

*

A guy with a clear conscience is one with a poor memory.

*

<u>Pray For Thy Enemy</u>
May the fleas of a thousand dogs infest the underpants of our enemies. May the bed bugs of a thousand beds infest their whole anatomy and make them kick their buckets soon.

*

Catholic: "I hate England. It's cold, wet and full of Protestants."
Protestant: "Why don't you go to hell? It's hot, dry and full of Catholics."

*

A girl falls in love and marries a guy who very much resembles her father much to the ire and consternation of her mother.

*

When does a husband feel threatened?
When all his good looking friends (half of them bachelors) start admiring his wife.

*

Sex is not the answer. Sex is the question. "Yes" is the answer.

*

Some women, after losing their patience waiting too long for the "right man" to come into their lives, get married. Others wait for the "right man" to come along, in the mean time, get married.

*

Why would a woman love her mother-in-law to be? Because she is a cash rich widow who could double up as a live in maid and a baby sitter.

*

When there is no death announcement in the newspaper obituary column continuously for three days, who gets worried?
The undertaker.

*

A newspaper advertisement - An undertaker for a husband. Any takers?

*

If a girl is dating an undertaker let her be forewarned that he's only interested in her body and not her soul.

*

Anyone who gives you the two cents worth of advice is one who is not worth a cent.

*

Never suffer alone. Get as many people as possible to suffer along.

*

Never suffer in silence. Let people hear you suffer till it deafens their ears.

*

If you are not wearing your panties don't climb a tree and get the dogs excited.

*

When is a woman half naked?
When she is naked below her waist.

*

What is the meaning of average?
Not as good as the good and not as bad as the bad.

*

What are bras?
Something many women buy to cover something they don't have.

What are bras?
Something many women buy to lift up a pair of something which droops.

*

What's a toothbrush?
Something old men and women use to brush something they don't have.

What's a toothbrush?
Something old men and women use to brush their dentures.

*

What is an orgasm?
A feeling that reaches the highest level of excitement and doesn't last long.

*

What's ecstasy?
A very happy feeling you have never felt before and last much longer than an orgasm.

*

Statistics of the past ten years show that 49% of those who are married are women and 51% are men including gays.

*

In a survey some men indicated that they preferred girls with slender legs and some said they preferred girls with fat legs. But the majority preferred something in between.

*

Why do party goers piss in the garden?
Because there is always someone throwing up in the toilet.

*

A sign outside a maternity clothes shop – "We are open on labour day."

*

A sign outside an optician shop – "If you don't see what you are looking for, you've come to the right place."

*

What is oral sex?
Talking about sex. To be more appropriate, a verbal discussion about sex.

*

When travelling to certain third world countries, tourists beware. Your luggage can be confiscated for not bribing the customs officers and you can be arrested for failing to bribe the police officers.

*

Never trust a husband too far nor a bachelor too near.

*

144

What do you do if a mad guy throws a grenade at you? Catch it, pull out the pin and throw it back at him and take cover.

*

An entrepreneur sees "tomorrow". The not so enterprising sees "today". A born-loser or a born-wasted broods over yesterday, remains idle today and is totally oblivious of a tomorrow.

*

Students dislike most of their teachers but they hate their maths teacher the most. He or she gives them too many problems. They feel depressed to have to put up with such a problematic person.

*

The couple's working life as well as their married life became very problematic because both happened to be maths teachers. They also ended up having three problematic children.

*

Teacher: "You were getting most of your sums wrong. But lately I've noticed that you are getting all your sums correct in your maths homework."
Student: That's because lately my father stopped helping me with my maths homework."

*

Looking at his son's report book, the father angrily said, "You have failed in your maths yet again. Now, give me a good reason why?"
Son: "I think it's because I have inherited too much of your genes."

*

A kid returns home from school looking very depressed and annoyed. He looks at his father and says, "Thanks for doing my maths homework last night. Now the teacher says I'm intellectually subnormal!"

*

Teachers are supposed to teach so that the students learn more. Instead, they end up trying to find out how much the students don't know by giving them too many class tests and homework.

*

What did the calculator say to its user?
You certainly can count on me.

*

What did the picture say to the wall?
First they frame me then they hang me.

*

If I tell you a joke about a post card which was not stamped, you'll never get it.

*

Not many are fortunate or rich enough to travel round the world. But no one realizes that whether rich or poor we all get a free trip around the sun every year.

*

A geologist is a person who buries himself in the study of the earth before he himself is buried in it.

*

What did one tomato say to the other?
You go ahead and I'll ketchup.

*

When does a horse have six legs and four ears?
When it's got a rider on its back.

*

What has two wheels and four legs?
A motorbike with a rider and a pillion rider.

*

There was a big hole found in the wall of a nudist club and the police are looking into it. Even the passers-by and perverts are looking into it.

*

A middle aged lady told her friend, "I have found at my age going bra-less pulls all the wrinkles out of my face."

*

It's simply a waste of effort telling a hair-raising story to a bald man.

*

Sam: "Have you heard a well kept secret about butter and jam?"
Tommy: "No"
Sam: "I'd better not tell you, you might spread it around."

*

Why is there always a wall round the graveyard?
Because people are dying to get in.

*

What happens when you jump into the sea from a helicopter?
You get wet.

*

How do frogs in China sound when they are on heat?
Cloak.

*

Why do you go to bed?
Because the bed doesn't come to you.

*

Why did Batman enter the pet shop?
To look for Robin.

*

The 82 year old Queen stopped attending Royal dinners because she couldn't control her hiccups, burps and farts and didn't want to end up issuing embarrassing Royal Pardons.

*

A filthy guy with a terrible body odour bought a skunk as a pet. But the skunk died after a few days unable to bear his stinking body odour.

*

Is the guy hiding in the drain a robber?
No, he's an undercover agent from the Special Branch.

*

The unruly kids in the neighbourhood play police and thief with real cops.

*

How can you write four 9's so that they equal 100?
99 + 9/9 = 100.

*

Ricardo: "I wanted to tell a story about an empty water tank but decided not to."
Wilkinson: "But why?"
Ricardo: "Because there's nothing in it."

*

Never ask a barber if he thinks you need a haircut.

*

Fred: "Last night a burglar broke into my house and before stealing anything helped himself with the food in the kitchen cooked by my wife."
Larry: "What happened then?"
Fred: "He died."

*

A big funeral procession was passing by indicating someone very important had died. A curious on-looker asked one of those following the procession, "Who died?" The guy replied, "The person in the coffin."

*

What can be possibly worse than having a television?
Not having one.

*

Alfred, seeing his friend Jason after so many years, asked, "How are you Jason. Who are you working for now?" Replied Jason, "The same five people. My wife and my four kids."

*

A lady guest asked her host, "How was my singing? Do you know I've spent $20,000 to learn how to sing?" The host said, "Just give me a moment." She then brought a male guest and introduced him to her, "He's a lawyer. He'll help get your money back."

*

Boss to his secretary: "Mabel, just because I cuddle you and kiss you passionately, who told you that you can laze around and not do your work in the office?"
Mabel: "My lawyer."

*

A rich lady went to the hospital to visit her injured chauffeur. She asked the nurse, "Is he badly injured?" "Yes. Are you his wife?" asked the nurse. "Certainly not. I'm his mistress." replied the rich lady. "Sorry, I've been given strict instruction to reveal his condition only to his wife and not to his mistress."

*

A sign outside a candy shop: - **"Sales Clerk wanted. Diabetic preferred."**

*

A sign outside a beauty parlour. - **"If you're 20 and want to look 40, that's your business. If you're 40 and want to look 20, that's our business."**

*

An aunt, disliked by Betty's parents was staying with them longer than they expected. One day she told Betty, I'm leaving tomorrow. Is that going to make you feel sad?" Replied Betty, "I'm already feeling very sad. I thought you were leaving today."

*

After seeing his report book the furious father asked his son, "Do you remember what I told you if you don't score good marks?" Replied the son, "That's funny dad. I too don't remember."

*

Mother: "If you are going to be naughty again, I'm going to call the police!"
Son: "If you call the police, I'll tell them we don't have a TV license!"

*

Little Tommy: "Mummy, can I have two pieces of cake please?"
Mum: "No problem, I'll cut it into two for you."

*

An American president described politics as the second oldest profession in the world and worse than the first.

*

Little Nancy on returning home from church with her father rushed to the kitchen and told her mother, "Mummy, do you know something?" The mother asked, "What?" Said Nancy, "There were four wakeupers in the church today." The puzzled mother asked, "Wakeupers?" Nancy eagerly said, "Yes, to wake up the sleepers and daddy was one of the sleepers."

*

A stand-up comedian's job can be a risky one. After an hour trying to entertain the audience with his disgusting jokes he can end up in hospital with a fractured skull. But joke book writers are save they don't encounter such a risk!

*

An absent-minded professor insisted, "I'm not absent-minded. In fact, I have an excellent memory. There are only three things that I can't remember. I can't remember faces, I can't remember names and I can't remember what the third thing is."

*

In a particular Caribbean highway one man is knocked down every thirty minutes and he's not happy about it!

*

What is a free gift?
All gifts are free, stupid!

*

A nervous old lady taking a plane for the first time asked the person seated beside her, "This is the first time I'm taking a plane. What happens if the plane runs out of fuel?" The cheeky guy told her, "We all have to get out and push the plane."

*

How do you get rid of varnish?
Take away the letter 'R'.

*

Why didn't any country win the World Cup in 1920?
Because the first World Cup was only held in 1930.

*

What kind of umbrellas do the members of the Royal Family in England carry when it is raining?
Wet ones.

*

If King Kong from America went to Hong Kong to play Ping Pong and died. Where will he be buried?
In a graveyard.

*

Is a doctor who treats a sick dog called a veterinarian or a vet?
No. He's called a dogtor.

*

Little Eunice, putting on a long face, told her mother, "When I grow up, looks like I'll end up marrying the boy next door!" The surprised mother asked, "Why do you say that?" Replied Eunice, "Because you don't allow me to cross the road and go to the other side to play with the other kids!"

*

The proud owner told her neighbour, "My cat won the milk drinking competition held in my club and he won his closest rival by six laps."

*

Who goes into a lion's den and come out alive?
A lion.

*

Some people think history was first written in Saudi Arabia because it's full of dates.

*

A rookie terrorist who was cornered by the police took out a grenade, pulled the pin and threw the pin at the police. The police who were nearing him ran away to take cover.

*

A shop owner was interviewing a guy who applied for the sales assistant's job. The shop owner asked, "Do you tell lies?" The job applicant replied, "No. I don't. But if it's a requirement, I can learn while on the job. I'm a fast learner."

*

Why is he always led down by his co-workers?
Because he is a deep-sea diver.

*

An old lady smiled at a little girl playing in the park and asked, "Do you go to school? The little girl with a sulky look said, "No, I'm sent!"

*

A student who doesn't do well in history strongly feels there is no need to have history lessons. He says, "Let bygones be bygones."

*

Another student instead of reading his history book reads the newspaper because history repeats itself.

*

At one time the people of France had to put up with a skeleton as the Emperor of France and the skeleton's name was Napolean Bone Apart.

*

John (a bachelor): "That's my daughter."
Smith: "John, that's Jason's daughter."
John: "Jason's wife told me I'm the father."

*

"Hello can I speak to Harold, please."
Manager: "Who is this calling?"
Caller: "I'm his grandfather."
Manager: "Harold took the day off to attend his grandfather's funeral."

*

A guy ran away from home when he was ten years old. Did his parents miss him? When he returned home after five years they didn't even know he ran away.

*

Which animal suffers the most when it has a sore throat?
A giraffe.

*

Which animal can be trusted?
A giraffe, because it will stick its neck out for you.

*

Larry: "Why do you look so bored? Have you been talking to yourself again?"
Henry: "Yes."
Larry: "I should say you are a very considerate person for not getting others bored to death!"

*

Judge: "Why did you hit the man with a chair?"
Accused: "Because the table was too heavy to be lifted."

*

The dumb Morris wondered how come his sister had three brothers and he only had two.

*

My father said, "You can't go to the X-rated movie, you'll see something you shouldn't. He was right. I saw my father in the front row."

*

Mother: "Janice, you are failing all your subjects. Look at your friend Valerie, she's always first in class. How is that so?"
Janice: "Because she has smart parents."

*

What gives you a sharp pain in your neck and then "you know not" what happened?
A guillotine.

*

Who was Lawrence of Arabia chasing in the desert?
The lovely Florence of Arabia.

*

When everything is coming your way, than you are driving in the wrong direction.

*

Antiques are things one generation buys, the next generation gets rid of and the following generation buys again in an auction at a very high price.

*

Gerald: "I'm an avid collector of antiques."
Derrick: "I know. I've seen your wife."

*

One person's trash (garbage) is another person's antique.

*

My bank just sent me a letter telling me it's the last time they will spend twenty-five cents to tell me I have only two dollars and fifty cents in my account.

*

"In our country, we like our liquor hard and our women soft."
"In my country, we like our liquor straight and our women curved."

*

"How did your mother find out you didn't take a bath?"
"I forgot to wet the soap."

*

To wear a bikini a girl must have the figure or the nerve.

*

You were the only survivor in the air crash. How come?
I missed the flight.

*

Benson: "I heard you taught your wife how to play bridge."
Rodney: "Yes and last week I won back half my salary."

*

Lamented a sad shop owner, "Business is so bad even the shoplifters are giving my shop a miss."

*

It's risky to sleep with your feet on your desk. You may lose your job.

*

A miser promised his sister that he would buy her a washing machine as a gift for her wedding. He bought her an Indian washing machine - a rock.

*

Do you smoke cigarettes?
What else can I do with them?

*

Dear women - After 45, your "get-up and go" has got-up and gone and you still never give up lying your age.

*

Women like jewels. The only golden thing they dislike is silence.

*

If infants enjoy infancy, do adults enjoy adultery?
The parties involved do.

*

While waiting for the right man to come along she's having a wonderful time with the wrong ones.

*

She dresses to kill but no victim till this day.

*

Why is the moon considered very poor?
It has no money and lives on borrowed light.

*

Most men wonder what women liked in men before money
was invented.

*

Character is what you are when there is nobody around.
You indulge in all the dirty things when there is no one
around.

*

You have the right to remain silent. Anything you say will
be misquoted then used against you.

*

Her female friends hailed her for making the wisest
decision. She married a fool who inherited a big fortune.

*

If ladies don't go shopping, all unwanted things will not be
sold.

*

When God created man he was still able to carry out his
routine tasks. The moment he created woman he became
spellbound and has still not recovered from the shock.

*

A wise man once said, "You can't kill a fish by drowning it. Similarly, you can't kill a bird by throwing it off a cliff. If you want to kill someone or some thing do it wisely."

*

Bachelors are happy to remain bachelors because they know more about women than married men.

*

Husband: "Why can't you appreciate a good husband?"
Wife: "I would if I had one."

*

He opened a flower shop – no luck. He opened a fruit shop – no luck. He opened a grocery shop – no luck. He then opened a jewellery shop and got 20 years.

*

A robber demands your money or your life but a wife demands both.

*

My wife objects seriously to my smoking. She says it's too expensive to have both of us smoking.

*

I love cats, they are tastier than chicken.

*

A wedding ring is the world's smallest handcuff.

*

A wise man once said, "If you wish not to see a fool, don't look into the mirror."

*

You don't need a good memory to tell the truth, but you certainly need one to tell lies.

*

There are so many religions in the world and yet all of them are united in worshipping only one thing - **MONEY**.

*

He is a bachelor but has fathered two sons and the shocking news is that his father was also a bachelor.

*

A man takes a woman to a room, removes the protection, sets the connection and increases the population. If too many men do it that leads to population explosion which is not happening in Singapore and Japan.

*

Why is sex so irresistible?
Because it's the centre of gravity for both man and woman where all the energy is stored which needs to be released regularly in order to avoid appalling or dreadful consequences.

*

In certain poor countries people eat in private and ease in public.

*

Men love challenges in life and women usually provide them.

*

Mathew: "I'm good at reading a person's mind and I know what you are thinking now?"
Ivan: "What am I thinking?"
Mathew: "Since you already know why should I tell you?"

*

Monologue is a conversation between husband and wife. The wife talks and the husband listens.

*

Dignity is one thing which cannot be preserved in alcohol.

*

A politician winding up his speech said, "I'm sorry for speaking longer than I was expected to because I forgot to wear my watch today."
A voice from the audience: "But there was a calendar behind you!"

*

What did the invisible man call his mother and father? Transparents.

*

A politician went on speaking for more than an hour non stop and an impatient audience shouted, "There's a bomb on the stage!" Startled, the politician jumped off the stage and started running for his life.

*

Never trust a dog to watch your food. Neither a cat.

*

A woman walking in the street wearing jeans and just a bra was talking to her friend on the hand phone and told her, "Do you know something. I forgot something and I can't remember what it is and I don't understand why everyone who passes by me is giving me that very funny look."

*

Father: "What would you like to be when you grow up?"
Son: "I want to be a military tank driver."
Father: "Wow, I'll certainly not stand in your way."

*

It is said that in Las Vegas many a gamblers lose all their money and have to beg in the streets to raise enough money to take a flight back home and according to the latest news the Las Vegas streets are getting more and more crowded with beggars.

*

Girl: "I can't go out with you at least for the next two weeks."
Guy: "Why?"
Girl: "I'm getting married tomorrow."

*

What do skeletons fear most?
Hungry stray dogs and bull terriers.

*

Whatever hits the propeller of an aeroplane, including birds, will not be evenly distributed.

*

A guy invited an acquaintance to his house for a drink. After having one too many, the guy pointed to the three photographs hung on the wall close by and said, "This is my first wife. She died of orange juice poisoning. This is my second wife. She died of lemonade poisoning and this is my third wife. She died due to a severe fracture on her skull."
Acquaintance: "How come?"
The guy: "It was all her fault. She was given two choices either to drink the orange juice or the lemonade. But she refused to drink either."

*

A boy with a toothache in a dentist's clinic said to the boy sitting beside him, "How nice if we were born without teeth." Replied the other boy, "In fact we are, they grow later."

*

A clear conscience is the result of a poor memory.

*

Steve: "I got this second hand car for my mother-in-law."
Gordon: "That's a good swap. But I wonder what those guys are going to do with her!"

*

Eye specialist: "Now read the letters at the top of the board."
Patient: "What board?"

*

Manager: "I have a funny feeling that the guy we recently employed is not honest."
Accountant: "Sir, you shouldn't judge by appearance."
Manager: "I'm not. I'm judging by disappearance!"

*

Alfred: "I really feel very sad. I just came to know that both my brothers are gays."
Edmond: "Doesn't anyone in your family like women?"
Alfred: "Yes, me and my two sisters."

*

Samuel: "Does your mother carry weights?"
Xavier: "Certainly not. Why do you ask?"
Samuel: "How else could she have raised a big dumbbell like you?"

*

A guy was passing by a dimly lighted street in the wee hours of the morning. A man who looked like a beggar approached him and said, "Sir, would you be kind enough to help this soul who is hungry and without a job. All I want is what you have and all I have is this gun," and pointed the gun at him.

*

A guy who always brags to his friends of having had sex with over a thousand beautiful girls told his friends, "You know something. My doctor has advised me to give up half of my sex life." An irritated friend asked, "Which half; talking about it or thinking about it?"

*

Why did the banana go to the hospital?
Because it was not peeling well.

*

Why don't they manufacture mouse-flavoured cat food?

*

What do you call a rotten essay?
A Decomposition.

*

Danny: "What are the names of your puppies?"
Tony: "Rickie and Vickie."
Danny: "Which one is Rickie?"
Tony: "The one next to Vickie."

*

Husband: "Do you believe men have better judgement than women?"
Wife: "I certainly do. You married me, didn't you?"

*

Sam: "Can you lend me $10, please?"
Roy: 'No."
Sam: "I was just joking."
Roy: "I wasn't."

*

First neighbour: "We'll be moving out soon. We're going to live in a better neighbourhood."
Second neighbour: "So are we."
First neighbour: "Oh, are you also moving out?"
Second neighbour: "No, we are staying right here."

*

Sherlock Holmes: "Watson, you're wearing a red underwear today."
Dr. Watson: "That's amazing. How did you know, Holmes?"
Sherlock Holmes: "It's elementary, my dear fellow. You've forgotten to wear your pants."

*

During a heated argument, the husband shouted, "You talk like an idiot." Replied the wife, "I have to, so that you can understand me!"

*

A young man filling in a job application form wrote under 'Sex': "Three to four times a week."

*

You said you are from a poor village and what you have done is to deprive your villagers of an idiot!

*

Judge to repeat offender: "What are you charged with this time, Mr. Jackson?"
Jackson: "I was just trying to get my Christmas shopping done early."
Police Officer: "Yes, before the store opened. Your Honour."

*

Mother: "John, you are always procrastinating. You must change."
John: "I will mum, I promise, form next month."

*

Alice: "Teacher, Doris took my pencil box and refused to return it."
Teacher: "Did you ask her nicely?"
Alice: "Yes, I did."
Teacher: "What did she say?"
Alice: "She told me to tell the devil that she took my pencil box. So, I came to tell you."

*

Judge: "What excuse do you have this time for stealing?"
Repeat offender: "I haven't thought of one yet. Can you give me time to think?"
Judge: "Very well, I will give two years to think."

*

Judge: "Aren't you ashamed of appearing in court again?"
Fearless accused: "I only come here once a year. You should be ashamed of yourself for coming here everyday of the week!"

*

SINFUL NOTICE
You must pay for your sins. If you have already paid, please disregard this notice

*

What do you lick and enjoy?
Ice cream.
What do you lick but don't quite enjoy?
Correct. So clever!

*

How do most men define marriage?
A very expensive way to get your laundry done free.

*

Men's belief: "Woman, without her man, is nothing."
Women's belief: "Woman, without her, man is nothing"

*

171

Impotence – Nature's way of saying, "No hard feeling".

*

Why did Robin Hood rob only the rich?"
Because the poor had no money.

*

The winter was so cold you can see a pickpocket with his hands in his own pockets.

*

Father: "My boy, I never kissed a girl until I met your mother. Will you be able to say the same thing to your son?"
Son: "I'm your son dad. I will certainly have no problem telling a big fat lie."

*

My children are finally grown up. My daughter has started to put on lipstick and my son has started to wipe it off.

*

Mothers of teenagers know why animals eat their young.

*

How many famous men were born in America?
None. All those born were babies.

*

In which month do women talk the least?
February.

*

Does a dentist know how to bake a cake?
No, he doesn't. His wife bakes the cake and he does the filling.

*

Good luck turns into bad luck when lightning misses you and strikes a nearby tree which falls on you.

*

Why do baby birds never smile?
Would you smile if your mother fed you worms for dinner every night?

*

Teacher: "If a man married a princess, what would he be called?"
Student: "Her husband."

*

On which side does an eagle have more feathers?
On the outside.

*

On which side does a bald man have more hair?
On the inside.

*

What do you get if you cross a cow with a duck?
Cream quackers.

*

What do you get when you cross a bed bug with a rabbit?
Bugs Bunny.

*

What is a porcupine?
A cross between a pig and a cactus.

*

What do exorcists do?
They scare the devil out of you.

*

Who can stop a huge speeding truck with one hand?
A traffic police.

*

What works only when it is fired?
A rocket.

*

What kind of dog says "Meow"?
A bilingual dog.

*

What do you call a deer with no eyes?
No idea (No eye deer).

*

What happened when the lion ate the comedian?
It felt funny.

*

Why was the cat near the computer?
To keep an eye on the mouse.

*

Why was the computer in pain?
It had a slipped disk.

*

Man: "Where there is a will, there is a way."
Woman: "Where there is a will, I want my name to be included in it."

*

Why do you feel you can easily make skeletons laugh for your jokes compared to human beings?
Because it's easier to tickle their funny bones.

*

What should you do if armed robbers break through your front door?
Run out through the back door.

*

What is bigger when it is upside down?
The number 6.

*

What is it that you can serve but cannot eat?
A tennis ball.

*

What goes through water but doesn't get wet?
Sun rays.

*

Between three and four in the morning people are sound asleep. If you want to steal your neighbour's newspaper do it during this time.

*

Two history teachers were dating and they always ended up talking about old times.

*

Which football goalkeeper can jump higher than the goal post?
All of them. A goal post can't jump.

*

What do they call Dracula when he umpires a cricket match?
Vampire.

*

Why do the business executive and manager look so bored?
They just attended a "Board Meeting".

*

Why did the team of fools who participated in the tug-of-war lose?
They pushed.

*

The two most common elements in the earth are hydrogen and stupidity.

*

A blockhead who saw the sign: "Man Wanted for Robbery" outside a police station, went in to apply for the job.

*

When a co-worker asked the intellectually subnormal guy why he had a sausage stuck behind his ear, he replied coolly with a smile, "I think I might have eaten my pencil for lunch."

*

Two lizards on the wall of a house were talking to each other.
First lizard: "Humans are very funny."
Second lizard: "Why do you say that?"
First lizard: "They spent a lot of money decorating their ceiling but then they walk on the floor."

*

Son: "Mum, are we having Aunty Shirley for dinner this Christmas?"
Mum: "No, it's turkey as usual."

*

A guy, who bought a parrot, brought it home and wanted to name it Ricky. So in order to train the parrot he looked at the parrot and said, "My name is Ricky." "That's funny," said the parrot, "so is mine."

*

A man who drives like hell bounds to get there sooner than later.

*

A mother had two lovely twin daughters who were both three years old. She then gave birth to a baby boy. When she returned home from hospital, her twins were admiring their baby brother. Suddenly, one of them asked anxiously, "Where is the other one?"

*

<u>JUST FOR LAUGHS</u>
Son: "Mummy it's over!"
Mum: "Good. Now turn off the TV and go and do your homework."

*

If you are a tasteless person and wished to become a cook, apply for the job in a government hospital.

*

If you are a very talented and capable person you know what to do. If you are not just do what you are told to do.

*

A blockhead: "Whisper those three words that will make me walk in the air."
Irritated girl: "Go hang yourself!"

*

Why do some men prefer love at first sight?
It saves them a lot of time and money.

*

Mrs. Jason: "This doctor is crazy over my daughter and keeps pestering her to marry him. But she doesn't like him."
Mrs. Simon: "Give your daughter an apple a day and that will do the trick."

*

Tom: "This is our family photograph taken with our dog."
George looks at the photograph and a bit puzzled asks, "Which one is your dog?"

*

A husband only sleeps with his wife. With all the other girls he's wide awake.

*

A 98 year old man proudly says that he doesn't have a single enemy in the world and laments that he doesn't have a single friend either. He has outlived them all.

*

Don't take life too seriously and work too hard. Relax and take life easy. After all, you're not going to get out of it alive.

*

Three old men took off their clothes and jumped into a river and had a good time. They then got out of the river and started dancing stark naked for a hot music. Just then a group of ladies were passing by. They couldn't take cover and two of them covered their private parts with their hands and the third covered his face. After the ladies left they immediately put on their clothes. Then the two asked the third guy why he covered his face. He said, "If ever the two of you bumped into any of these ladies in future they'll recognize you, but they won't recognize me unless I get to sleep with anyone or all of them."

*

Who say happiness is the only thing in life?
Bachelors.
Who say happiness in not the only thing in live?
Married men.

*

A happy marriage means marrying a very obedient woman who can cook and do all the household chores. She must be very rich and good in bed. But the sad thing is the law doesn't permit you to marry three different women.

*

Some women dress to kill. They cook the same way.

*

A wise man once said: "Don't wear a thick make-up. You have the right to be ugly. Why abuse the privilege."

*

Variety may be the spice of life but monotony happened to be the way of life for most married man.

*

To steal ideas from one person is plagiarism. To steal ideas from many is research.

*

Those who **can** are doers. Those who **can't** end up being consultants.

*

You can wear a nice perfume but don't marinate in it even if you didn't have your shower for weeks.

*

Tour guide to tourist: "The people in this town are very healthy and live beyond 100. They don't know what a cemetery is." The tourist said cheekily, "Give me a double barrel gun and a spade and I'll show them what it is!"

*

A psychiatrist is called a shrink because that's what he does to his patients' wallets.

*

Practice makes a man perfect. Since no one is perfect, why practise?

*

When I was a child my family was so poor that the only thing I got on my birthday was a year older.

*

If a husband pampers his wife then he's an old man married to a young lady. If a wife pampers her husband she is easily 30 years his senior!

*

Smart man + smart woman = romance
Smart man + dumb woman = pregnancy
Dumb man + smart woman = affair
Dumb man + dumb woman = marriage

*